WAIT

Erica Allaire

Published by

Hot Ink Press and Steamworks Ink

Imprints of CHBB Publishing

The right of Erica Allaire to be identified as the author of this work has been asserted by him/her in accordance with the Copyright, Designs and Patents Act 1988.

No part of this publication may be reproduced, stored in a retrieval system, or transmitted in any form or by any means without the prior written permission of the publisher, nor be otherwise circulated in any form of binding or cover other than that in which it was published and without a similar condition being imposed on the subsequent purchaser.

Cover art by: Rue Volley

Edited by: CLS Editing

Copyright © 2015 Hot Ink and Steamworks Ink

DEDICATION

This book is dedicated to Laura A. Ring: friend, sister, and partner in crime. My life is brighter because you are in it.

ACKNOWLEDGEMENTS

Too many people helped in the development of this book for me to have any chance of naming them all. I'll do my best, and hope the many others will forgive me.

During the research for this book, particularly in the subjects of race and slavery in 1825, I am greatly indebted to Natalie J. Ring and her many friends and colleagues on Facebook who gave me suggestions for more books to read than a good college course on the subject would probably have used.

While writing, the support from my beloved husband and children was invaluable. My first draft of this was a marathon conducted as a sprint, and culminated in a fourteen hour forced death march at the end when I just HAD to finish it. That I emerged reasonably well nourished, hydrated, and still married is a minor miracle.

My first readers, Anna L. Smith, Charles Schultz, and Pamela McNamee, were wonderfully supportive and wonderfully prompt with encouragement and suggestions. Fellow CHBB author LaQuette was kind enough to read my novel and point out language with unintended connotations. Pamela McNamee also did a final run through after my revisions, catching errors and inconsistencies, and Susan Bianculli corrected my French . All remaining errors, obviously, are mine.

I was unable to find a picture that was quite what I wanted for this, so I turned to Ed Bergman of Bergman Photography. He introduced me to talented makeup artist Crystal Lee and to incredible model

Taylor Woodard who makes a perfect Grace. Grace's dress was made by the wonderful Michelle Neveux. Last but certainly not least, the setting for the photo shoot was the Sarah Gibson house. Thanks to Sean Mahaffy for introducing us to the wonder and charm of this building.

Finally, I have to thank the CHBB family for love, support, and making all of this a pleasure.

Chapter One

The ship groaned as they changed direction. *A few degrees to the south*, Grace thought, although, in the windowless cabin, it was hard to tell.

From the bed opposite hers, Charlotte moaned softly and sat up. "Remind me again why we didn't just take the air ship?"

Grace smiled. "There have been seventeen assassination plots uncovered in the past decade, Your Ma—Cousin."

"Right. Assassins. Why don't they ever show up when you'd welcome them? Morning sickness or sea travel? No, it's always at some grand entrance when you're actually enjoying yourself for a change."

The young queen was paler than usual, and her light brown hair was bedraggled, but her smile was the same as it always was. Grace suspected that it was that smile, more than her progressive policies and courage, that made Charlotte the most beloved Monarch in several centuries. The policies, though, likely accounted for the assassination attempts.

There was a knock on the door, and Charlotte moaned more convincingly while pulling down her veil. Grace went to the door, her gait steady after weeks at sea, and opened it carefully.

Mrs. Potter held out two steaming cups of tea. "I thought you and your great aunt might like some, given how raw the day is."

"Mrs. Potter, you are an angel," Grace declared, taking the cups carefully. "Aunt Elizabeth will be grateful, as am I."

The woman smiled, her middle-aged face pink. "Both Lady's Maids, all three seamstresses, and two of the hairdressers are too sick to leave their bunks, so I've got the undermaids seeing to them. Even so, I've so little to do, without the queen present. I understand her schedule was too tight, and she had to take the airship, but I'll be glad when we get to Boston, and I can take care of her properly."

"I'm sure she'll be glad, too, Mrs. Potter," Grace assured.

Mrs. Potter pulled the door closed, and Grace carried the cups across the shifting floor to her cousin. Charlotte lifted the veil and took her cup with a sigh.

"I hate lying to her, but she can't keep a secret to save her life."

Grace sipped her own tea, strong and with a hint of bergamot. "Well, she loves the story of Aunt Elizabeth, and I know Aunt Elizabeth loves being able to help, even if only by being impersonated. After being born with a crooked spine and told you'll never live to grow up, it's something to have been a diplomat, spy, author, and notorious recluse."

Charlotte laughed softly. "I'm positive she saved my life, talking Leopold and me out of letting the doctors bleed me when I was pregnant. They'd tried that on her so many times, and she assured me that it only made one sicker."

Grace shuddered at the thought. "All of England would have mourned. Let's be honest. Not one of your uncles would make a decent king. Least of all Father."

"They would have been better if they'd been allowed to marry who they wished. That was a stupid law, and I think it kept them all from growing up." The queen shook her head. "Although, it was hard enough to get Parliament to agree to change it to only the heir being bound by the monarch's decision."

Grace settled back on her bed as she finished her tea. "Well, Father would never have married my mother anyway. He wouldn't even have acknowledged me if she hadn't died birthing me while he was still infatuated."

Charlotte turned her free hand palm up as though in apology. She didn't need to say anything. Royal dukes didn't marry opera dancers, not even English, white skinned opera dancers.

Grace looked at her hand, mahogany brown against the white porcelain of the cup, and spared a thought for the French dancer that had been called The Divine Night in both countries. Prince Augustus had thought that she had been born somewhere in Africa, but he hadn't been sure. He knew that she'd spoke only French and English, and had had no memory of any life before Paris, growing up a dancer in a world where a woman with no family had few better options in life.

Would I have been a dancer, too, if she'd lived? Would that be better, or worse, than a Royal bastard?

There was a faint cry from on deck, followed by another she could make out.

"Land ho!"

There was another faint lurch in the ship, and Grace took a breath but didn't move to stand. She was careful not even to glance at her royal cousin, trapped behind the veil and alibi.

Charlotte chuckled softly. "Oh, go on up, Grace. There's no sense in both of us missing it."

Grace dropped a kiss on the queen's brow. "You are a saint, Cousin. I fear I am not, because I'm not going to tell you no."

Another soft laugh echoed as she crossed to the door, not bothering with a coat, despite the chill. She'd briefly gone up on deck most days, desperate for a breath of fresh air. After weeks of open water and open sky, she was just as frantic now for the sight of something new. Land. America. Perhaps, if the navigation had been incredibly accurate, Boston.

She took the narrow stairs at a run, bursting out into the air and immediately moving to the spot she had discovered at the beginning of the voyage, just to the left of the companionway. No ropes crossed there, no seamen ever seemed to need to be just there, and it was close enough to the side for a fair view.

Land was only a smudge on the horizon, but she stared at it, her breath catching. America was strange, rough, wild…new. It was vast, far larger than England, and much of it was occupied by natives with multiple cultures and languages of their own. Canada, to the north, was bizarrely a different country, as Grandfather had seized it from the French two generations before, and the two adjacent territories had never melded as one might have expected.

There was another cry, and a ripple of emotion from the crew as something on land was identified, but she couldn't, for the life of her, understand what it was. She stopped a boy scampering down from the crow's nest. "What is it?"

The boy, a lad of perhaps eight with freckles and a gap between his teeth, grinned at her. "It's Boston, Miss! The captain done it, straight across without an hour out of our way!"

She hugged the news to herself, watching as the blurred horizon slowly took shape. The steeple of a church on a hill, other ships in the harbor. The October sun was warm, cutting through the wind, and she turned her face up to it.

"Lady Grace, where's your bonnet? This rough air and sun will ruin your complexion!"

Grace turned to face Mrs. Potter, herself properly attired in spencer and bonnet, and a gurgle of laughter escaped before she could stop it. "There are many things in life I need to worry about, Mrs. Potter, but that isn't one of them."

Mrs. Potter blushed red. "I'm sorry, Lady Grace. It's habit, chasing after royal girls for this long. But still, your skin is lovely in its own way, and you ought not to risk harming it."

She gave a reassuring fib about not staying out much longer and went back to her gazing. A flock of geese flew over the land, and sea birds had come out to greet the new ship, their harsh cries like a welcome. It was impossible to tell at that point if they were the same or different from the birds she saw at home, but she still looked and wondered.

Unless she became a spy or a diplomat like Great Aunt Elizabeth, this might very well be the only trip she ever took outside England. Oh, if this visit went well, Charlotte might make another in a few years, here or to Canada, or even to India. However, unless it was covert again, she would probably have to take one of her more respectable ladies in waiting. The queen was quite good at withstanding social pressures, but there were limits.

The wind was driving them in, a boon for the last part of their journey, and it seemed no time at all that they were having to slow within the harbor proper. Sailors from other ships called out to theirs, greetings and news, and they were close enough to make out individuals. There was a collection of buildings, primitive for London or even Bath, but larger than she had expected, and carriages pulled by horses instead of machines. The roads were in poorer condition, she remembered. Only the most expensive machines could handle them.

The *HMS Griffin* slid through the harbor waters like a knife through butter, smooth as silk as it pulled into port. There were men on the dock scrambling forward to catch ropes and make them fast, and she watched the way they jumped and turned, an intricate dance joining land and sea. Snippets of French mixed with the English, likely Canadians from the north. She fought to hide a smile as a blond fellow let loose a string of French about the state of one of the ropes another had just been swinging from.

Voulez vous morir? Do you want to die?

It was time to go back down, to help Charlotte get ready to disembark, but she lingered a little, watching them. The blond man was good looking enough to be a London fop if it weren't for the tan and muscles he sported from honest work. She wondered idly if his eyes were blue or brown, and if he would still be good looking close up. Most men weren't, making people watching more enjoyable than actually meeting them.

A cry from above alerted her, and she looked up to see a heavy tackle swinging loose. Time stilled so that it was like a physics lesson. She watched the trajectory that would bring it unerringly into her own skull with mild surprise that her muscles were frozen, and yet, she felt no fear. However, she was snatched up in a pair of tan arms, swung off the ground by another rope as the tackle crashed where she'd stood a moment before.

His eyes are blue, she thought, *and blazing. He is even better looking close up.* He smelled of sweat, soap, and pine, and he looked as if he was going to kiss her.

There wasn't time for the luxury of disappointment that she couldn't allow such a thing to happen, although she'd doubtless feel it later. Instead, she looked back into his blue eyes with her brown and spoke crisply and clearly in French. "Voudriez vous mourir, monsieur?" She used the formal, *Would you like to die*.

He smiled as he set her back on her feet, a flash of white teeth in the bronze face, and bowed. "Mademoiselle."

"*Merci, Monsieur. Je suis reconnaissant.*" *And she was grateful, but not grateful enough to kiss him.*

"*C'est rien.*" He smiled more deeply. "*Anges vous protègent.*" *Angels keep you,* she translated.

She was glad her complexion rarely showed a blush. His smile seemed to say that he was well aware that she'd wanted that kiss as much as he had, but he had respected her refusal. Heavens knew, not all of her dance partners had been as well behaved.

She smiled again so that it was not quite running away to turn and go back below decks. He had work to do, after all.

So did she.

****

The metal brace that was a necessary part of Charlotte's public disguise was unwieldy and not terribly comfortable, but the young queen never complained. Of course, Grace reflected, they both knew that was how Aunt Elizabeth lived every day, just to be able to stand.

With the braces, Charlotte creaked when she moved, and the metal at boot and wrist was the first thing anyone noted, even before the black veil that hid her features. It marked her as old, infirm, and wealthy enough not to mess with.

"Once more," she murmured as Grace gathered her bags and marked her own for the crew to send to the governor's mansion.

"Once more," Grace agreed.

Another knock on the door, and the veil went down again. Mrs. Potter took the metal bound hands in her own. "Princess Elizabeth, I do wish you'd come to stay with us at the governor's mansion until your train tomorrow. It would be so much more comfortable for you and Grace."

Charlotte waved a hand weakly. "Too many people," she murmured.

"We'll be fine, and I'll be back tomorrow night, only a few hours after the queen arrives," Grace reassured her. "Once I get Aunt Elizabeth settled with her friends, I'll take the next train back."

"I'm worried about that too, but you're as stubborn as your Aunt is." Mrs. Potter seemed to draw up her courage and stood taller. "So I brought you this."

"This" was an Electric Coil disruptor pistol.

"Where did you—" Grace began.

Mrs. Potter held up her hand. "Fathers can be forgetful. I wouldn't be surprised if your father doesn't even remember he leant this to you for your trip."

Grace glanced at Charlotte behind her veil and accepted the gun. It was a finer model than she was used to but fit into her hand as if she'd been born with it.

"Thank you, Mrs. Potter," she said sincerely and impulsively leaned forward to embrace the woman. "I'll see you tomorrow night."

The sounds the braces made were impressive, as was Charlotte's stately passage up the stairs and out on deck with them. Grace adjusted her own hat as the wind hit it. With coat and hat, she was far more daunting, and so less likely to inspire kisses, but the gun was a welcome weight in her pocket.

There was no sign of the blond dockworker, but the lad from the crow's nest took one of the valises from her and called a horse-drawn cab. The cabbie took the remaining bags, coins were shared, and she sank back into the upholstery with a little sigh.

"Fresh food first or bath?" she asked.

"Bath first. Then lunch. Then another bath." Charlotte tried to stretch and raised the veil with a grimace. "I truly hope I have completely over reacted and that Evelyn will tell me so when we rendezvous. Then, perhaps, we can take the airship home, after."

"Having your assa—um, trained assistant handle any threats is prudent. But yes, that would be wonderful."

Charlotte reached out and patted her hand while the arm brace whirred its protest. "I can't tell you what a comfort to me having you here is, Grace. You're sure there's no one I've pulled you away from for the little season?"

Grace snorted. "I've no interest in getting married for my money and connections to someone who will overlook my breeding and skin color for royal favor. Two impoverished viscounts, three middle-aged wastrels who already have heirs and spares, and some extremely ambitious Cits. Not everyone finds their true love, Cousin. If Leopold has an illegitimate half-brother somewhere, well, let me know."

Charlotte brightened immediately at the mention of her husband of the past decade. "I'll ask, but I think his father was more…um…"

"Restrained? Faithful?" Grace shook her head. "I suppose they do make men like that, somewhere."

The steady drum of metal shod hooves on cobblestone was soothing, the swaying of the carriage much like the ship. Grace peeked around the curtain for a glimpse of the new city. The streets by the docks were narrow, with rough wooden buildings, warehouses, and shipping yards. The smell of fish was almost hidden by the sea air, but the sewer system was more primitive than she was used to, a definite note that lessened as they moved into the city proper. Streets widened, gas lights appeared on corners, and stone and brick buildings replaced wood.

It was a tantalizing glimpse, but in only a few minutes, the cabby had drawn up in front of a fine stone hotel with a liveried man waiting to help them down and take their belongings.

****

The hotel was fine enough for minor royalty, and quick enough to please anyone not a complete hair-for-brains. Within thirty minutes of their arrival, two baths had been brought in and filled with hot water. An assortment of towels and perfumes were left beside each, and the staff had backed away to leave them in peace.

"I feel as if I've run away on holiday," Charlotte confessed. "No pomp or circumstance, no hangers on, and no sea sickness. I'll actually be able to enjoy food again."

"Make a list of what you'd like, and we'll divide it between lunch and dinner," Grace advised. "You deserve one day of actual vacation."

Sometime between the discussion of pasties and tarts, the water finally grew cool. Slipping from the bath, Grace wrapped a towel around herself and held one out for Charlotte. "Clothes or dressing gown?"

"Dressing gown. We'll be eating in here, anyway." Charlotte sighed as she wrapped the silk robe around herself. "If Leo and the children were here, this would be Heaven."

Grace tied her own gown and stepped over to the window. It was bright sunlight out, and peering around the window, she looked out at the chaos of a Boston day. A boy with a handcart was selling roasted nuts to passersby, and a ragged child was selling papers. People walked to and fro, with horse drawn carts and carriages rumbling down the street's center. A man stepped out of a building that looked like a pub, and her breath caught in recognition. It was the man from the docks. He wore a jacket, hiding the muscles but not the tan of his face or the smile.

It was a fine area for a dockworker to be in, even at a pub, but perhaps he'd had a delivery to make. He certainly strode off with no sign of tarrying.

She couldn't help watch until he was out of sight.

Chapter Two

They had cut things rather close, as the airship was due the evening after their arrival, but Grace was amazed at how smoothly it all went. At ten o'clock the next morning, her day bag was sent off to the governor's mansion, while a taxi was called again for her to take 'Aunt Elizabeth' to the train station. By 10:15, according to her watch, the taxi was pulling up to the train station, and she and Charlotte were handed off. The creaking, whirring metal was very much in evidence, just as they wanted them to be.

Grace carried the two bags, waving off offers of help, and headed straight for the nearest official, Charlotte in veil and whirring beside her.

"Excuse me, sir, is there a private necessary room for my aunt to use?" she asked.

The man, a ruddy complexioned fellow of middle years, tipped his hat to her and the obvious expense of their clothing. "Right over there, miss, reserved for ladies." He checked the watch that hung on a fine chain from his waistcoat. "It's twenty after ten. What time is your train?"

"Not until eleven," Grace assured him, smiling.

He tipped his hat again and smiled back.

The necessary room was small and primitive but sufficient for their needs. Grace stripped the metal braces from her cousin, changed the feathers on her hat and put it on Charlotte over the veil, and traded her own coat for a poorer, slightly ragged garment suitable for a maid with a not-terribly generous employer. A quick adjustment of her hair took it from a formal updo to a knot at the back of her neck. A quick check in the mirror confirmed that they had gone from frail elderly woman and her fine relative to sturdy middle class widow and her servant. With braces and coat stowed in the bags, they looked completely different and far less remarkable than the pair who had arrived.

She cracked the door, looked around quickly, and then held it for Charlotte. After the other woman strode past her, purposeful and strong, Grace scurried to keep up with the bags.

The same official stood directly in their path, and Charlotte paused.

"Need a taxi, Madam? And does your girl need help with your bags?"

"I'm sure she can manage," Charlotte said dismissively. "But yes, a taxi would be welcome."

"You there, boy. A taxi for the lady!" The man turned away to another traveler, and they followed the boy to a taxi, Charlotte handing out coins imperiously.

When at last they were safely inside the taxi with the windows drawn, Charlotte pulled back her veil and gave a shaky laugh. "I was positive that man was going to recognize you. He'd talked with you not ten minutes before!"

Grace settled back and shrugged. "It wasn't that great a risk. White people almost never pay attention to your face when you're dark skinned. It's your clothes and your bearing they notice."

Charlotte looked shocked. "Grace, that can't be true."

Grace snorted. "Dress me up as a housemaid and set me to dusting, and my own father will walk past me without recognizing me. He has, twice. It's how I get out of social engagements I absolutely can't stand. The servants still recognize me, certainly, but no one else ever has. And that's because servants are taught to notice expressions, so they pay much closer attention to faces than people who don't have to worry about being struck or fired."

Charlotte sank back against the cushions. "That's terrible. Like you're not even a person."

Grace smiled. "If it makes you feel better, the same thing happens to anyone who is very poor. Dress poorly enough, and no one wants to make eye contact with you, as though poverty were contagious."

Charlotte shook her head. "We'll change the world, Grace. I'm just constantly appalled to find how much it needs changing."

The park they were headed to was, ironically, named Princess of Wales, after Charlotte in her younger years. It boasted the only airship landing area in Boston proper as well as gardens, a walkway beside the River Charles, and numerous stone and brick out buildings as well as a wooden pavilion that rivaled those at Covent Garden. The cabbie let them down there without comment, and there were hundreds of people about as they turned down one of the loose stone paths. Flower sellers and food sellers dotted the place, and the scent mixed frying food and greenery over the tang of the river and the hint of sea air.

They walked without talking, Grace three steps behind, following the directions both had memorized. A roundabout route took them to a small building just behind the airstrip, and Charlotte brought out the key and unlocked the door.

"Our home for the next several hours, I fear."

The building was square and squat, perhaps ten paces across. Metal shutters let in some light through the leaded panes inside, and it was possible to peer out between the slats without risk of being seen. There were wooden chairs inside and a locked chest that yielded cushions for them as well as several bottles of wine, medical supplies, a remarkably fine tool set, and several guns. Grace unloaded the bags into it, dusted the room carefully, and then helped Charlotte out of her widow's garb, which hid the type of white dress Charlotte favored for grand entrances. Beneath her veil, the crown-like arrangement of her brown curls was intact, and Grace threaded white silk flowers in amongst it.

"There. Now you are ready for the great switch."

Charlotte laughed. "I must admit that part of me enjoys this as much as Aunt Elizabeth does. If only it were just a lark, and not necessary…and I'm still not sure it is. But if it is, then Evelyn is putting herself in danger for me, and I hate that."

"And she loves that. Evelyn has been training for this since she was a child, and she chose it. She is ten times more able to take care of herself than even Aunt Elizabeth, and we won't talk about the skills she has and is perfectly happy using on your behalf."

Charlotte nodded and then sighed. "Being queen means that even my ideals are only freely mine if they serve England. To have someone kill on my behalf in war is bad enough, but to have someone go out and kill for me without that uniform is worse. Yet, I know if I'd let her kill Napoleon ten years ago, when she'd had the chance, Europe might be at peace today. It was the wrong decision on my part, whatever morals prompted it."

Grace sighed and set up the cushions on the chairs, gesturing for the queen to sit before she did. "And perhaps Napoleon would just have been replaced with someone else. Your decision to go after his Navy and Airships, to the exclusion of all else, safeguarded England and undoubtedly saved thousands of English lives. He can't get to us, he knows not to bring his airships over the channel, and he has no more fleet. Yes, he took Spain, but it's not as if the Spanish were ever reputable allies."

She reached into the chest for the smaller valise and picked it up. "So, cards, chess, or embroidery? It's a trifle dim in here for reading."

At some point the area outside became more crowded, although their spot behind the landing field was still cordoned off. A marching band began tuning up in the distance, and mounted police began to patrol between the people and the landing fields. Afternoon sunlight was still coming in through the slats when the gaslights in the park went on.

The plan, devised with Evelyn and known only to Prince Leopold and the three of them, called for a veiled Evelyn to come down the gangplank, which turned to the side and at one point hid her from view. At that time, Evelyn would trade off with Charlotte, who would continue down and throw off her veil to greet the crowd. Charlotte was famous for grand entrances, making it unlikely that anyone on the ship would object to her going out first. She'd also cultivated the habit of appearing veiled when not at her best—usually during morning sickness from her three children—and no one questioned the practice. It was as simple a plan as they could devise, and Grace tried not to worry.

There were cries from the crowd outside. The airship had been sighted. Grace put away the chess set and picked up the veil to cover Charlotte. Evelyn would be joining her in the stone building, and both would have to wait some time for the crowd to die down before leaving.

"Are you ready?" she asked. It was a stupid, reflexive question, because when was Charlotte not, and did it even matter if she wasn't. Charlotte never had a chance to answer anyway, because that was when the explosion hit.

The sound was deafening, a roar like the heavens had split open, and then screams from the crowd joined in. Running to the windows, they saw the ball of fire that had been the airship, the wreckage flying down onto the air pad with pieces landing among the crowd. The band screeched to a halt in a flurry of notes, and police struggled to control their panicked horses.

"My God." Grace swiveled back to look at her cousin, but the queen was already turning away from the window. "What are you going to do?"

"Do?" Charlotte asked, her eyes flashing. "They've murdered seventy people to get to me, and they'll receive no satisfaction if I can help it. We'll mourn the dead later. For now, it's time to see what my people think of the divine right of royalty and how much attention they pay to the anthem. Stay here and meet me at the governor's mansion when you can."

A great cloud of dust and smoke obscured the wreckage, but Grace watched with her breath held. A thread of wind parted the smoke, showing a white figure standing in the midst of the landing pad while smaller pieces of crashing wreckage landed around her. Most of the screaming cut off abruptly into an almost eerie silence, and then the people nearest Charlotte fell to their knees. The band raggedly started up again, joining into God Save the Queen, and Charlotte held out her hands to her people. Grace winced as a flaming ember landed not a foot from the young monarch, but Charlotte never flinched.

"My people," she called out as the band finished. "I am grieved to come to you in this manner, saved by the heroism of the airship crew and passengers and the grace of God. There was treason most foul, and we will dwell on that tomorrow. For now, know that I am here, that I shall not fail you, and I shall not abandon you."

There was a new roaring, and the people rushed to the barrier, but not beyond it, while the police didn't even try to stop them. Snippets of Charlotte's clear, carrying voice still reached Grace as Charlotte went along the line, touching hands, asking if any of the crowd were wounded, and delegating people to see to their care. It was an eternity before she allowed the governor's delegation to lead her away from her people and to a carriage, and Grace stepped back from the window and sank into the nearer chair.

Seventy people, murdered. Most of them were people she'd known since childhood. Evelyn was one of the few people both she and Charlotte truly counted as a friend.

"I don't know how, Evelyn, but I'm going to find the people who did this," she promised the empty air. "And when I do, they're going to pay."

****

It was several hours before she felt safe to leave the outbuilding without attracting notice. She wore her fine clothing again, with only a reticule in her hand. The gun was a comforting weight in her pocket, and she locked the chest before slipping through the door, locking that behind her, too.

There was still a faint haze of smoke in the air, making the gaslights look like glowing oases in the gathering dark. She walked briskly along the nearest path, watching the people who still trekked through, many leaving offerings of flowers around the airship pad. At one of the gaslights, she saw a finely dressed woman arguing with a man who looked familiar. Stepping closer, she confirmed that it was the dockworker, although he was better dressed than he had previously been. She turned her gaze to focus on the woman, noting blonde hair, a sharp chin and pert nose, and dark brows. The woman looked up at her suddenly, as if sensing her gaze, and Grace turned away, certain she would recognize the woman if she met her again.

Why would someone who could afford good clothing pretend to be a dockhand? She discarded the idea that he had stolen them because he had smelled of soap, earlier, which should have alerted her at once that he was not what he seemed. Much of the royalty she knew didn't bother with it, although she conceded that her father and Prince Leopold both knew how to bathe.

He had been there, on the ship that brought them in. He had been near their hotel later the same day. Then he was at the location where Charlotte would have died if not for their ruse. That made him suspicious, and by extension, the blonde woman as well.

She reached a taxi with no unpleasantness and directed it to take her to the train station. She'd take another from there to the governor's house. Charlotte would need someone with her who knew the truth.

Heavens knew that she needed that, too.

****

The butler at the governor's mansion looked at her dubiously when she appeared with no maid and no baggage.

"I am Lady Grace, daughter of Prince Augustus, Lady in Waiting to my cousin, Her Majesty Queen Charlotte of Britain, the Americas, Canada, and half a dozen other places I can't be bothered to name right now. Her Majesty has need of me. Are you going to detain me further, or do your job and direct me to her?" Grace felt it was totally unnecessary to mention that she was the *illegitimate* daughter of Prince Augustus. She still technically outranked the governor, let alone his butler.

"I'm sorry, Lady, right this way," the poker faced gentleman deferred. "Mrs. Woodward is with Her Majesty at the moment. She acts as hostess to the governor, as he is unmarried."

The butler was, perhaps not surprisingly, English. She pondered that as he led her back to a room in the rear of the house.

"Your Majesty, I just don't think that you should be alone at such a time," a voice was saying when the butler cleared his throat and knocked upon the door.

"Enter," Charlotte's clear voice called.

She sounded at the edge of impatience, and Grace grimaced in sympathy.

The butler opened the door. "Lady Grace to attend Her Majesty."

Charlotte greeted her with a smile and turned to the older woman beside her. "There, you see, Mrs. Woodward, We shan't be alone. Our cousin will be here beside Us. We are grateful for your concern but must retire to Our chambers now. No doubt We will see you on the morrow."

Grace kept the smile firmly on her face, but winced internally. Charlotte only pulled out the royal 'We' when thoroughly displeased.

"Mrs. Woodward," she murmured, inclining her head politely.

"Lady Grace," the older woman replied, nodding in return.

She was moderately resplendent in blue silk in a fashion that Grace recalled from the previous year and was white haired, plump, and nervous as a hen with one chick.

"If you are sure then, Your Majesty…."

"We are," Charlotte replied serenely, and the older woman had no choice but to bow her way out.

As soon as the door closed behind her, Charlotte turned to Grace and leaned against her. "I need my bed chamber and a bath. Could you make it happen?"

Grace hugged her firmly. "I will. You hide in here, and I'll come get you when all is ready."

There were times, Grace reflected, when it was better to be illegitimate. If her parents had married, she'd have to worry about being only four lives away from being a completely public figure, needing to guard every minute of emotion, and needing to be strong and serene when she wanted to scream.

She found Mrs. Potter ready and waiting to supply all of the queen's needs, including privacy. Within a quarter hour, a hot bath had been carried up to the queen's chamber, and Grace shooed the servants out as she welcomed her cousin in. When the door was shut and locked, she turned to her cousin.

"There. It's safe to cry now, as long as you need to."

Charlotte's smile wobbled and then broke apart into violent sobbing. Grace held her a few minutes, then helped her into the hot bath, sitting beside her in companionable silence until the sobs at last had stilled.

Chapter Three

Mrs. Woodward, it turned out, was something of a snob for an American. Her father had been the younger son of a duke, her husband likewise the grandson of an earl. In England, she would have been considered a pillar of polite society, one step below those with titles. In America, of course, no one cared.

She was pleasant despite that small vanity and pressed Grace to eat a proper American breakfast of apple pie, cheese, steak, and eggs. Grace did her best, aware that she was, if not eating for two, then definitely socializing for two. Her Majesty, she had explained to her hostess, had the megrims that morning and would need to stay to bed a bit, but would be certain to be present at the evening meal.

Unfashionably early by British standards, supper was to be only eight people, a small gathering until Her Majesty had had time to recover from the trip. A grand ball, Mrs. Woodward confided, was scheduled for the following Saturday.

Finally, Mrs. Woodward confessed that she ought to leave for late services at her church. Grace was too tactful to inquire if it were the Church of England, given that few in America attended such. Instead, she reassured the woman that they would be quite comfortable while she was gone. She watched her off, folded a piece of pie in a napkin for Charlotte, and headed up stairs.

Charlotte was delighted with the pie, and more delighted with the news that their hostess had decamped. "Excellent! It is bad of me, for I know she is a good woman who means only well, but she wears on me. And this will allow us to sneak off and pay a morning call."

Grace chuckled. "Well, you recover quickly. You can't miss supper, you know, even if it is at six in the evening. Mrs. Woodward would certainly cry."

Charlotte grimaced. "I know, I know, but there are two people here who I'd really like to meet without her supervision, and this is a prime opportunity." She threw off her dressing gown and gestured to the wardrobe. "What do we have that says restrained good taste?"

Grace shook her head but went to make the selection. Time, after all, was passing, and Mrs. Woodward's services wouldn't last all day.

****

The address Charlotte gave the driver was only a few streets away, an equally splendid neighborhood on rather higher ground than most of the city. The butler who answered the door was younger and less poker faced than the one at the governor's mansion and clearly recognized the queen, although he attempted to hide it.

"Mrs. Hanover and Miss Fitz George to see Mr. and Mrs. James, please," Charlotte said with pleasant firmness.

"Certainly. Mr. James is from home, but I can bring Mrs. James to you?" he offered, looking relieved at Charlotte's nod. He showed them to a pleasant morning room done in beige and green and went to find his mistress. The door failed to latch properly, and they could hear his conversation clearly.

"Mrs. James, there's a Mrs. Ha-hanover to see you, with a Miss Fitz George," he said, stumbling a little.

The woman who answered sounded annoyed. "I don't know anyone by those names. Must they call today? I have inventory to go over, and the new production line starts next week."

"Mrs. James, you really must—" the poor man protested, and the woman sighed.

"I know, I know, all part of having married David. Of course, I'll see them, but it's not as if the blue prints will design themselves. Why people waste time paying social calls to strangers is beyond me."

They heard brisk steps headed in their direction, and Grace saw that Charlotte was having as hard a time keeping a straight face as she was. All of polite society in London knew that "Mrs. Hanover" was the name the queen used when visiting incognito, while "Fitz George" was the surname used by the acknowledged Royal bastards. Apparently, that knowledge didn't extend to America.

The door swung open to reveal a pretty, brown haired young woman with spectacles perched on her nose and a smudge of ink on her forehead. "Good morning, ladies, I'm—oh, Good Heavens!"

She sank into an awkward curtsey, and Grace hurried to shut the door behind her as Charlotte pulled her back to her feet.

"None of that, Mrs. James. Mrs. Hanover is visiting you today, and no one more important than that."

The young woman shook her head. "I don't know what I'm supposed to do," she confessed. "May I offer you a chair? Would you like tea?"

"Yes to both," Charlotte said soothingly, seating herself as their hostess rang a bell and spoke softly with someone at the door.

Mrs. James paused again as she came in. "Am I allowed to sit, as well? And I'm sorry, am I supposed to know who your companion is?" She turned surprisingly sharp eyes on Grace. "You have the same eyes, though different coloring. Are you related?"

Charlotte and Grace both laughed. "Yes," Grace replied. "I'm Lady in Waiting to Her—to Mrs. Hanover and her cousin as well."

The woman clasped her hands. "Oh, did your father marry an African princess?"

Grace coughed, hiding another laugh. "Not exactly. Fitz George indicates the grandchildren of King George the Third without benefit of, er, wedlock."

"Oh." Mrs. James seemed to consider that for a moment, then nodded. "Well, I'm very pleased to meet you both, and I'm not nearly this scatterbrained in the normal way of things."

Charlotte drew her out with questions about her work—she apparently designed automatons, and had not given it up when she married. By the time the tea tray arrived, she had warmed up a great deal and had asked them both to call her Verity.

"I've only been Mrs. James for a month now, but I've been Verity my entire life."

They talked of inconsequential matters over tea, which came complete with cucumber and butter sandwiches, ginger cookies, and scones. The jam was made from cranberries, which were like black currants, but tarter and bright red. Only when they had finished did Charlotte fold her hands and regard Verity with a steely look.

"Now, Verity, I would like to hear the story of how you and your David managed to uncover an assassination plot against me."

Verity blushed. "The whole story? I mean, the real...that is—"

"I think," Charlotte said gently but firmly, "that you need to tell me everything."

She did. It was a harrowing story of hoodlums, a masked hero who turned out to be a respectable member of society, and more than a few parts that trailed off with the suggestion of romance and intimacy. The end, though, didn't lead to as much information as Charlotte had clearly hoped.

"So the villain of the piece died in jail without implicating his co-conspirators? Hanged himself?"

Verity hesitated a moment. "To tell you the truth, I very much doubt that he hanged himself. He'd neither the courage nor the competence to fashion a noose from his clothing. I suspect he was murdered by people afraid of what he might reveal."

Charlotte nodded slowly. "I can see why you didn't tell the whole story to the authorities. It's certainly safer for both you and your husband if your part in this does not seem too great."

Verity sighed with relief. "Yes. And truly, David doesn't *want* to be knighted."

Charlotte shook her head. "My dear, the queen never grants a knighthood for anyone's pleasure. It is always and only for the good of the realm."

Grace hid a smile at Verity's look of consternation. "You get used to it," she advised gently. "These times when she gets to be just a woman, like us, they're a type of holiday for her. Because, underneath it all, she is always, first and last, the queen."

Chapter Four

The grand dining room at the governor's mansion had a table that could seat forty when all leaves were in place. With it sized to eight, the room seemed vast, with empty space on all sides that even the well-trained servants seemed to find a trifle intimidating.

Grace didn't take as much time as she might have to appreciate the size and slightly overdone gilt décor of the room. From the moment they had gathered for the meal, she had been interested in one of the guests to the point that she struggled to hide it. In addition to the governor and Mrs. Woodward, Statesman Charles Adams, Statesman Benjamin Franklin Jr., and Captain Alfred Johnson of the local militia were in attendance. However, Grace's true attention was sealed to Viscount Fansworth's daughter, Sophia Farnsworth, who was visiting family in the colonies. She also happened to be the very same woman Grace had seen at the airship pad.

Charlotte, as queen, sat the head of the table. By rights, with eight guests, their hostess should have taken the foot. Instead, she had seated the governor on Charlotte's right, and herself to the right of him. The captain had Charlotte's left, with Miss Farnsworth on his left, which left Grace at the foot with Mr. Franklin on her right and Mr. Adams on her left. This allowed her to watch Miss Farnsworth quite naturally, and manners allowed her to keep it in check.

Mr. Adams was either less versed or less concerned with manners. The salad course had barely commenced before he had started addressing comments, questions, and entreaties to the queen.

"America is a new land. It needs a new way of ordering itself," he told her.

Charlotte nodded sympathetically to the first several gambits, but then held up her hand. "Mr. Adams, I hear and understand your concerns, and I promise that I will meet with you to discuss them more fully. This, however, is neither the time nor the place. Let us enjoy this fine meal that our hosts have arranged for us and speak on more tranquil matters."

After that, Mr. Adams spoke very little, applying himself to his food instead. He was a square faced man with a fringe of white hair around a bald dome, looking uncomfortable and not at all happy to be there. Grace tried to ask him polite questions, but was grateful when the salad course gave way to the soup—an American dish called clam chowder—and she could talk with Mr. Franklin.

Mr. Franklin was older, stouter, and far more agreeable than Mr. Adams. He left his shoulder length brown hair loose, although Grace suspected that he dyed it. He also managed to flirt outrageously and indiscriminately with both his seatmates without ever once being unpleasant. Even better, he gave her a whispered hint as the servants collected the soup plates.

"Ask him about his farm, his wife, and his children."

Sure enough, questions about his farm in Quincy drew Mr. Adams out, and she was able to give him half her attention while listening to Mr. Franklin's conversation with the mysterious Miss Farnsworth.

She learned that Miss Farnsworth's mother was French, that she loved to dance but could not sing fit for an audience, and that she had two younger brothers and one older back in England. Still, Mr. Adams smiled at her warmly at the end of the fish course, so she felt she'd done her duty by her hostess and Charlotte.

Mr. Franklin eyed her keenly when she turned to him at the start of the poultry course. It was a mild curry dish, a nod to the extent of Charlotte's empire, and she recommended it to him when he seemed disinclined to start. He laughed, softly, and took a bite, but did not look away.

"You'll make a diplomat or a diplomat's wife," he said. "Make people comfortable, get them to talk, listen more than you speak. Did they teach that to you, or did it come naturally?"

Grace lifted an eyebrow, not quite offended, then gave in and smiled. "I'm both the daughter of a royal prince and a bastard, Mr. Franklin. A certain skill with diplomacy is crucial if one wants even a somewhat comfortable and ordered life."

He snorted, loud enough to draw looks, but waited for the gazes to turn again before speaking. "If you wanted comfortable and ordered, you wouldn't be here. I think you'd better consider what it is that you do want out of life and go after it. I'd wager on you to get it."

She merely smiled and turned the conversation to his writing. The meat course consisted of venison marinated in maple syrup, a strange but wonderful combination. Grace passed it with talk of Mr. Adam's wife and children. The dessert course—too many to even try, although Mr. Franklin managed— she spent talking about Mr. Franklin's inventions, and she made note of what to pass on to Charlotte. Mr. Adams was earnest and eloquent but blunt. Mr. Franklin was brilliant and could charm snakes out of trees.

Oh, and by the way Your Majesty, I think Miss Farnsworth must be a spy.

After dessert was finished, Charlotte rose and invited the men to linger over a glass of port if they so wished, although all had risen to their feet when she had.

"Ah, the torment to be forced to choose between fair spirits and fairer companies," Mr. Franklin lamented, a hand over his heart.

Charlotte quirked a smile at him. "Mr. Franklin, it is frequently and mistakenly thought that the time men spend over their port is for their benefit. In truth, women prefer to have a restoring cup of tea before continuing on with your foolishness."

He staggered a little as though struck. "Your Majesty wounds me. In truth, I will comfort myself with a glass and give you the brief respite from our male folly that you command."

Mr. Adams looked exasperated, the governor tolerant, and the captain perplexed, but all continued to stand as the ladies left the room with Grace at the back to close the door.

Charlotte laughed aloud. "Well, he is a card, certainly. Thank you, Mrs. Woodward, for inviting him."

Mrs. Woodward smiled. "He is a rascal with the ladies, but you can trust him to know proper boundaries at a dinner party."

"If not in other environs?" Charlotte quirked an eyebrow. "And, Miss Farnsworth, it is good to see you again. I haven't seen you since your presentation three years ago."

Miss Farnsworth curtsied. "Thank you, Your Majesty. I am surprised that you remember me."

Charlotte gestured her to a chair. "I try hard to remember every young woman presented to me. You are the ones who are most going to change the world. Men are easily distracted by wars and politics. Women know what is important...making the world a better place for our children to inherit and making our children worthy of such an inheritance."

Miss Farnsworth sat, her expression surprised. "So does that mean that wars and politics should not concern women, Your Majesty?"

Grace snorted in spite of herself, and Charlotte smiled.

"We all must deal with war when it comes, and politics is eternal. But we must not ever believe that those are ends in themselves."

Mrs. Woodward fluttered her hands. "I'm sure I'd rather not deal with either, begging Your Majesty's pardon. Shall I call for tea?"

With only the four of them, conversation remained general, and Grace admired the way Charlotte drew both Miss Farnsworth and Mrs. Woodward out about themselves. Miss Farnsworth's mother had left France to marry her father before the Terror, and she had no family remaining there. Mrs. Woodward had three grown sons and one granddaughter, although her oldest son's wife was pregnant, and she was hoping for a grandson. She was a widow, and Miss Farnsworth had had two seasons, but did not feel ready to marry.

Grace might have thought that it was just a coincidence that she had seen the woman with the mysterious dockworker, but there was a certain tension in the younger woman that she distrusted. One which became more pronounced when the governor led the gentlemen to join them.

"Why don't Mr. Franklin and Mr. Adams sit on either side of me, so that I may get to know them better?" Charlotte asked in a veiled command.

The governor looked from Grace to Miss Farnsworth—seeming to look longest at their bosoms—and sat next to Grace, a hair closer than politeness would dictate.

Governor Spencer, Grace's briefing had told her, was a Tory, unmarried, something of a libertine, and politically, at least, the queen's enemy. That he had been the one to order the arrest of the villain caught plotting an assassination attempt on Charlotte did not reassure her. After all, that man had also died while under the governor's imprisonment.

He was, however, a fairly small fish compared to the sharks she'd learned to swim with. She deflected his conversation with polite but persistent questions and reverted his gaze from her chest with frequent references to the artwork around the room. There was a lot to choose from, since it was arranged in what someone had imagined was the Chinese style—in red and gold, with knick knacks, statues, scrolls and paintings everywhere.

Still, when Charlotte requested that Miss Farnsworth play the pianoforte and that Grace sing, it was something of a relief. They agreed on "Greensleeves," a fairly uncontroversial song that both knew without sheet music.

Watching Miss Farnsworth's long, slender fingers dancing over the keys, Grace reflected that Evelyn had had very similar hands and a similar playing style.

Did they have more in common than that?

Chapter 5

"First, let's start with the list of groups who want me dead."

Grace groaned. "It might be faster to list the groups who *don't* want you dead."

They were both sitting on the queen's bed in their dressing gowns, and Charlotte hit her idly with a pillow. "Pay attention. There's the entire Tory party, the American Separatist Movement, the Irish, Scottish, Australian and Indian Separatist Movements. Why is it that Wales and Canada cause me so little misery? Then there are the factors outside our empire. The French, certainly. What remains of Spain, but they'd be foolish to waste resources on me instead of the Corsican. Possibly anyone involved with the slave trade, since we destroyed the French fleet and also destroyed three-quarters of the slaving ships in the world. Then there are just the anarchists who want things to be complete chaos with no government at all. Did I forget anyone?"

Grace sighed. "The families or lost loves of anyone who's ever been executed for treason or transported to Australia."

Charlotte shook her head. "There's money behind it, so I doubt that there's a single family at the root, unless it's ours." She laughed at Grace's look of shock. "Yes, none of my uncles want it, none even has a legitimate heir, but otherwise, I'd put them rather high on the list. It happens in royal families all the time."

Grace closed her eyes and leaned back against the mattress. "So, there's money. Verity's . . . What, Uncle in law? . . . was promised money and power. Miss Farnsworth is half-French, and meets a dockworker, who transforms into a respectable gentleman, and who I think is also native French from the way he speaks it. But blowing up the airship…that probably came from England. There was no missile, so whatever blew it up was already on board, waiting for a very clear, very public place for your death to be witnessed. So, right now, the only people I trust are you, me, and Leopold. And Aunt Elizabeth, bless her metal braces."

Charlotte nodded and yawned. "Enough for tonight. It's a web, but we'll unravel it."

"And if we can't?" Grace asked.

Charlotte's eyes became very, very still. "Then we set fire to it and watch who runs for cover."

****

The clicking noise woke her. It was as soft as knitting needles, but a little too fast, and too many needles. She reached under her pillow, where she kept the disruptor pistol when she slept, and took the safety off before she pulled the chain to ignite the gaslight.

A dozen fist-sized metal spiders scurried in her room, with a dark figure spearing them one by one with a dagger. He moved so silently that she still only heard the click of the spider's legs and the slight crunch as he staked one.

Acting on instinct, she turned the pistol on the closest of the spiders instead of the man. The zap froze it but didn't seem to harm it, and the man reached over to stab it before going on to the next target. After that, it became a kind of dance. She shot one close to him, he stabbed it while it was still, and she picked another target and started again. The process was surprisingly silent. The Electric Coil was as quiet as his dagger, with just the burst of light to announce each shot.

When he staked the last spider, however, she turned the pistol firmly on her rescuer. Somehow, she was not in the least surprised to see that it was her dockworker dressed in the tight-fitting black of a professional thief.

"I think, monsieur, that you and I need to talk."

He smiled easily, teeth white in his tanned face. "You're not going to shoot me."

She shot the dagger out of his hand. "I wouldn't count on that."

His grin widened, and he nodded. "A talk would be lovely, mademoiselle."

He settled down on the end of her bed, both hands in plain sight. "I swear, I mean no harm to you or your mistress. On the contrary, my interests are most definitely served by your queen remaining alive, healthy, and in full possession of all her territories."

She seized on that last. "And what territory is so essential to you?"

He shook his head, still smiling. "We all have secrets for those we love and serve."

She nodded slowly, accepting the limit for the moment. "And so," she prompted, gesturing at him with the pistol."

"And so, I went to the dockyards where your queen's staff was arriving, to see if anyone among them was one I knew to be a spy. And, instead, I found a beautiful young woman who didn't think getting saved from having her skull crushed was sufficient introduction for a kiss."

"She still doesn't," Grace affirmed. "And?"

"There was no one I suspected there. Later, I came to watch your queen land and saw . . . well, what we all saw. I don't know how she survived, but I most fervently thank God for it."

He seemed sincere, but Grace had been of marriageable age for seven years. She especially distrusted sincerity. "And?" she asked.

"And, since then, I have been watching your queen's lodging, waiting for something to happen. Tonight, two men released these at the window to this room. I had a choice between following and attacking them, or destroying what they had set loose. I chose this."

The gun almost wavered as she thought, but she willed her wrist steady. "So do you know what they are?"

He nodded, for once with no hint of a smile. "They are death. They would have killed everyone in this house if they were not destroyed first."

She imagined that, the giant spiders clicking their way from room to room, and shuddered. "You've seen them before?"

He nodded. "Once before."

"Do you know who sent them?"

"Not directly, but I know who invented them, who probably manipulated someone else into buying and using them. Napoleon."

Her breath caught, and he smiled again.

"Have I earned enough to keep my life, then? You and your queen are safe for another day."

"Why do you keep saying my queen?" she blurted. "Surely she's your queen, too?"

He shook his head, still smiling. "I already have a queen. It's difficult for a man to have two. Now, are you satisfied?"

She shook her head. "What's your name?"

He laughed, a low baritone sound that reached to her toes and made her again regret the kiss that had never been. "That . . . that is worth much more than my life. A kiss at the very least. Next time we meet, you may tell me if you still wish to know." He rose to his feet and bowed to her. "Goodnight, my lady. Sweet dreams."

He turned as though whether she shot or not was no longer of interest to him and headed back out the window. She stared after him for a long moment, and then snorted.

"I may dream, but I seriously doubt that they'll be sweet." Getting up, she gathered up all the ruined spiders one by one, along with the dagger he hadn't retrieved after she'd shot it. Locking them in a drawer, she shook her head. "Charlotte is not going to believe me in the morning."

Checking that the safety was again on, she returned the pistol to its place under her pillow, and touching it, was eventually able to sleep again.

Chapter Six

The trip to see Verity was Charlotte's last escape from her title and her duties. By the next morning, a ceremonial guard had stationed themselves around the governor's mansion. They were, Grace learned, volunteers who had decided to do so without orders, and quite possibly, without permission. It would make a second attack by automaton spiders far more difficult, of course, but it also made sneaking out of the house quite impossible. Which, of course, made it all the more tempting.

The politics of the house were decidedly mixed. The governor and his valet were not openly against the queen, but the rest of the servants, who were all American, besides the butler, quite openly distrusted them. Where the butler's loyalties laid remained an open question.

The royal servants—a modest ten in number, with Mrs. Potter in charge of them—were received fairly happily by the American servants for their connection with the queen, while Grace was accorded a respect only one step short of awe. Her Majesty, of course, could not have been more revered if angels had followed her blowing trumpets. Mrs. Woodward, however, was treated with a respect strangely devoid of warmth, which made Grace wonder if she were one of those people who were pleasant among fine company and dreadful to the servants when no one else was about.

"Do you think your Frenchman talked the guards into coming?" Charlotte asked when they had a moment alone. "It's a nice thought, and certainly most welcome in the circumstances, but do you think English soldiers would have thought of it?"

Grace paused a minute in thought. "Thought of it, yes. Then they would have brought it up to their sergeant, who would have brought it up to the lieutenant, who would have brought it up to the captain. . . ."

Charlotte laughed. "Americans seem more spontaneous in a lot of ways. Less disciplined, I suppose, but really it is hard to fault them too much for it."

They had decided to keep the spiders a secret for the time being. "It's always better to keep your enemies wondering," Charlotte had told her. "Let them tie themselves in knots of supposition, while we seem blissfully unaware."

Still, Grace so much wanted to discuss the devices with someone who could tell her more about them. She could paint, sing, sew, and shoot, but she had no training at all in the making of automatons. She rather thought Mr. Franklin would have some ideas, but although she liked him, she didn't entirely trust him. The natural person to ask was Verity James, but they hadn't even officially been introduced yet. It was enough to make her want to scream.

Instead, she kept Charlotte company through an interminable series of morning calls. Cards were brought up, and to each and every one, the queen had announced that she was, indeed, at home. They had met with silly rich women more interested in their dresses than themselves, earnest and plainly dressed women hoping to catch the royal ear, and awed subjects, who could barely string a sentence together. No one paid much attention to Grace, any more than to the footman at the door—a comment on her dress, or on his uniform.

The only time Charlotte was ever anything other than pleasant and gracious was at close to two in the afternoon. Two of the awed type were present, sipping tea and seeming to count the minutes to the proper quarter of an hour, when they would make their leave. The butler announced Mrs. Anders, a very beautiful, somewhat overdressed red head whose brocaded train was carried by a small dark child in a matching uniform. He stumbled a little carrying it, and the woman reached out and slapped him without pausing in her conversation.

Charlotte set down her cup with an audible *clink*. "Madame," she said icily. "May I remind you that a true lady never strikes a servant, let alone a child."

The woman looked at her, perplexed. "Oh, he's not a servant, Your Majesty. He's a slave. I bought him last month when I chose the fabric for this dress."

Charlotte ignored her to kneel down beside the child, who still held the train in both hands, only a stray tear showing he'd been struck. "Are you all right, child?"

He stared at her, not blinking, and Charlotte rose again.

"You may send me the bill for him, Mrs. Anders. He'll be staying here from now on."

"But, Your Majesty, I have no wish to sell—"

"Perhaps We were not clear, Mrs. Anders. We will be removing this child from your care. Our offer to make financial restitution to you is independent of that and will not be made again. Have We made Ourselves quite clear?"

The two awestruck ladies appeared to try to shrink further into their seats, and Mrs. Anders paled, and curtsied.

"Your Majesty."

"We thank you all for your visits, but We will be retiring now."

She nodded to the footman, who immediately opened the door. The ladies rose at once, bobbing curtsies, before fleeing. Mrs. Anders managed to make her exit less of a retreat, but Grace was pleased to see that she looked more frightened than angry.

More enemies, what else do we need?

As soon as the door closed, Charlotte knelt down by the boy again, who stared at her with something like terror.

"Grace, help me."

Grace obediently came and knelt beside her, eye level with the child. He looked six or seven years and sturdy enough not to have been starved.

"My name is Grace. Can you tell me your name?"

He looked at her a moment, then at Charlotte, who nodded encouragingly.

"It's safe to talk. No one will hit you here, I promise."

He looked again at Grace, as though she looked safer. "Joshua."

"I'm pleased to meet you, Joshua. Did you have any family at Mrs. Anders's house?"

Charlotte said an extremely unladylike word under her breath. "I hadn't thought of that."

Joshua shook his head. "Ain't got no family."

Grace gave a small sigh of relief. "This is Queen Charlotte. She's my cousin, and she's very nice. She wants to find you a home in one of her houses, where you can learn to read, write and figure, and grow up to be a free man. Would you like that?"

Joshua looked dubious at the learning part, but nodded.

"Good. Then I'm going to introduce you to Mrs. Potter, who helped to raise me when I was little and helped to raise Queen Charlotte too. She'll find you a bed, more comfortable clothes, and food."

She held out her hand, and Joshua paused only a second before putting his into it.

After Joshua had been placed in Mrs. Potter's capable hands, Grace tracked Charlotte down in the queen's bedroom. Shutting the door behind herself, she folded her arms and looked at her cousin.

Charlotte threw up her hands. "I know, I know. I lost my temper. I overstepped my bounds as queen and may have broken the Constitution. And I don't care."

"Charlotte, you can't buy them all. There are a million and a half African slaves in America. Even if the trade is illegal now, there's more being born every day, almost certainly faster than they're dying."

"I know. But, today, I could buy this one. Tomorrow . . . tomorrow we'll figure something out for the rest."

****

The incident made Grace pay more attention to the invisibles. It was not that there were no dark skinned people in Boston, but that most of them were in positions where her class had little cause to notice them. One of the stable hands was a free black man, as was one of the men who came to clean the gaslights. One of the flower sellers who frequented the street was a black girl of sixteen or so.

All of the soldiers outside and all of the guests that came in through the front door were white.

Joshua also gave Grace an excuse to go down to the kitchens. It was a refuge she had discovered in her father's house as a child, and in every grand house she had lived in since. The kitchens were where servants were able to speak plainly to each other. She hadn't tried to gain acceptance there—it had seemed too much an imposition—but with the shy child now adopted by the entire household, she was eagerly welcomed. For whatever reason, and she was fairly certain it came down to the color of her skin being so close to his own, Joshua felt most secure when she was near.

"Have you thought of having any of your own?" Mrs. Carson, the housekeeper, actually dared to ask her the second day she snuck down to keep him company at his breakfast.

Grace paused, a spoon of porridge half way to her lips. "I hadn't," she confessed. "I've never met a man I was willing to grow old with, children or no children. And without that, I don't want to bring more children into the world."

Mrs. Carson shook her head. "It's a good thing to be picky, miss, but there's such a thing as too picky."

Mrs. Potter paused, overhearing the comment as she supervised the making of the queen's breakfast. "A good provider may not be enough, nor a handsome smile, but if you hold out for perfection, you'll likely end up alone."

"Or, perhaps, married to someone like Prince Leopold," Grace teased. "The queen seems happy enough."

Mrs. Potter snorted. "She didn't find perfection. She found a good man with faults she could accept because of his virtues." She winked at Grace. "And if you repeat that to Her Majesty, I will deny it, for all we all know it's true."

Grace laughed, mock threatening them with her spoon. "No more matchmaking. It's too early in the morning."

After the debacle with Mrs. Anders, they had not accepted further uninvited guests. Charlotte met the following afternoon with both Mr. Adams and Mr. Franklin, listening to their concerns for a good two hours. Or, as she had told Grace afterwards, Mr. Adams had shared his concerns, while Mr. Franklin reworded them more tactfully.

"For all that Americans don't hold with hereditary titles, power does tend to run through families. Mr. Adams is the son of the famous Mr. Adams, who averted a massacre back in the '70s and championed the rule of law when relationships with the colonies were quite tense. His brother, Quincy, is a delegate to Parliament, so two of the sons went into law and politics. As for Mr. Franklin, it appears that his charm is inherited. I hear that Mr. Franklin Sr. seduced a courtier's daughter while in France and was caught by none other than Marie Antoinette, who declared that she was delighted to arrange a wedding immediately. The girl returned to France for a visit and perished in the Terror, leaving the younger Mr. Franklin to grow up in the image of his father." Charlotte shook her head. "I can just imagine the scene. I've heard so many stories of the French queen, although she's been very quiet in her exile. I'd love to see her, but it wouldn't do to draw attention to her."

Grace quirked an eyebrow. "She's only two hundred miles away. With good roads, that would be a long day's journey with mechanical horses. Here, of course, it would likely take a week. And wolves on the way, if what I hear of Maine is half true."

Charlotte laughed. "Yes, Maine by rights should be part of Canada, although it wouldn't do to say so in front of residents of either place. I hear there are a few small towns trying to pass as cities, but most of it is still wilderness dotted with farms. It would be lovely to travel over it by airship, just to see it, although the nearest airship pad would be Montreal."

They both sobered at the reminder of the recent loss, and Charlotte shook her head and forced a smile. "You should go let Milly dress your hair before dinner. We're expecting at least one pleasant couple tonight."

"The Jameses?" Grace guessed.

Charlotte nodded. "This way, we get to officially meet them before Saturday's ball. I may have to pull Royal Privilege and only attend for part of the evening. I wouldn't hesitate in England, it would be expected, but I rather hate to here."

Grace patted her hand as she stood. "Why don't you make a grand entrance after the bulk of the guests have been greeted? That will certainly be understood, and even admired, and will spare you the first hour at least. As long as you warn Mrs. Woodward of your plans, she can send you word when it is time to appear."

Charlotte nodded. "That sounds wise. Is it odd of me, to wish for the relative peace of sea sickness?"

Grace chuckled. "Having never experienced it, I really can't say."

It *was* pleasant to have someone else brush out her hair for her. Milly was theoretically Grace's lady's maid, but, much of the time, she simply dressed herself. Helping Charlotte, instead of allowing one of the servants to do it, was an accepted part of her role as Lady in Waiting. It also allowed the queen time alone with a confidant as well as emphasizing the royal rank.

Grace watched in the mirror as Milly pulled through the black curls. Her mother had had tiny, tight curls by the one portrait she had of her, and her father's hair was straight as a board. Her curls looked as if they had come fresh from an iron, reaching to her waist when allowed free rein and long enough to sit on if held straight. Grace didn't protest when Milly fashioned it up in an intricate knot with a curl hanging to each shoulder— a fancier style than she usually chose.

"There. If you like it like this, I can do the same for the ball. Or I could do something really special."

Since 'really special' likely involved objects woven into the hair—someone had worn a model ship on her head recently—Grace assured her that the current style would be perfect.

"I'll just add flowers, then, on Saturday. Let me know when the queen decides what colors you and she will wear, and I'll order them. Silk, likely, since America seems not to have caught on to hot houses yet."

Mr. Adams, Grace vaguely recalled, had one on his farm, but used it to grow orange and lemon trees. She smiled at the girl. "That will be lovely, thank you. I'll be sure to ask the queen what she would like."

The night's guests did indeed include the Jameses. Verity had removed both spectacles and ink smudges for the event and was dressed in a green evening gown that made her look both lovely and far more ordinary. It was a relief to see the humor flash behind her brown eyes. Her husband was tall, blond, clean-shaven, and a pleasant spoken man she had trouble imagining wearing a mask, picking locks, or rappelling off rooftops. Then, Grace caught his expression when he looked at his wife, and revised her opinion. Appearances, apparently, were deceiving.

Besides the governor and Mrs. Woodward, there were four other guests. Mr. Watts, a young man of moderate social presence and no strong politics, was the great-nephew of the Prime Minister, Lord Liverpool. Given that his great uncle was one of Charlotte's major obstacles, this reassured Grace only mildly. The other three, however, were a complete surprise, as none were white, and two were darker than she.

The Reverend Thomas Paul was a Baptist minister, a man of middle height, graying hair that thinned at the temples, and skin the color of black coffee. His teenage daughter, Susan, a pretty girl with wide and thoughtful eyes, accompanied him. With them came the reverend's protégée, a tall, slender man Grace's own age, Alexander Twilight, whose skin was only a shade or two darker than Mr. Watts. It reminded Grace that Lord Liverpool was part Indian on his mother's side, and raised the question of what made society declare one white or colored.

The queen had not yet joined them in the drawing room, and Mrs. Woodward passed out small glasses of cordial, which Miss Paul declined with only the smallest hint of regret. Introductions were made, and Mrs. James drew from Miss Paul that she was very fond of music, which allowed some easy conversation while they waited. Grace used the time to predict the seating arrangements, which would depend on Mrs. Woodward's opinion of everyone's social position.

No one sat, so there was no need to rise when the queen was announced, although all present hastily set down their glasses. Susan looked nervous, although her father looked as comfortable as if he'd been invited to give a sermon. Grace wondered how much more nervous Verity would be if it were actually her first time meeting the queen.

Grace was unsurprised to find herself near the bottom of the table, where Mr. Watts was seated in the theoretical position of honor. She was to his right, with Mrs. James across from her on his left. Mr. James sat next to his wife, and Mr. Twilight next to Grace, with Susan and her father completing the side on the queen's left, and Mrs. Woodward and Governor Spencer on her right.

Mr. Twilight was well educated, with a beautiful baritone voice and an honest interest in her opinions that was refreshing. Looking at him, she had to wonder if someone were matchmaking. Sadly, although she liked him, she was no more attracted to him than to the rather pompous and silly Mr. Watts. It was annoying, given that Mr. Twilight was just the sort of man she might have been willing to marry, had there been a spark. She found herself wondering if there might have been a spark, it she hadn't been almost kissed by a French thief.

As course followed course, she found herself wishing that she'd kissed him and gotten it over with. Likely, she'd have forgotten it by then if she had.

The ritual of tea with the other ladies in the drawing room was a pleasant interlude that felt rather less formal without the gentlemen present, and the more so as Mrs. Woodward excused herself. Verity invited both Susan and Grace over to her house for the following afternoon to see her newest invention.

"While I would be honored by your presence, Your Majesty, I know how many demands there are upon your time."

Charlotte sighed. "I would have enjoyed it. But, yes, the delegations from both the Pennsylvania and Virginia colonies are due to arrive tomorrow. I will be meeting with both of them. The fifteen colonies all have concerns, and I've promised to meet with all of them during the weeks I am here."

"You would be very welcome to visit my house for our poetry reading Friday night," Susan interjected. "It is much less grand and very informal, but we have at least four people reading this week."

"Two days gives Mrs. Woodward time to even out the numbers if you wish to miss dinner here, Grace," Charlotte commented. "I can't, of course, but bring me back word and any books that are available."

"I can pick you up in my carriage on the way," Verity added. "I think that sounds lovely, and David is busy that night anyway."

It was all arranged before Mrs. Woodward returned from her errand, and Grace felt a guilty lightness at the thought of two outings from the governor's mansion in the following two days. She turned a rueful smile at Charlotte, who returned it with perfect understanding. They were both bound by their duties, but that didn't mean that escape wasn't something to savor.

Chapter Seven

Grace was unable to get Charlotte alone the next morning, so brought up her thought as circumspectly as she could while Charlotte was having her hair done. "I was thinking of asking Mrs. James for suggestions about that pest problem we discussed previously."

Charlotte glanced up at her. "I think that is a reasonable idea," she said slowly, as though examining the thought for flaws. "Yes, why don't you."

With that permission, Grace secreted one of the deactivated metal spiders into her reticule under a handkerchief and a bit of knitting. The pistol, as always, went into her jacket pocket. She seriously doubted that she'd be willing to give it back to her father when she returned to England.

They took luncheon alone, except for the servants going in and out, and Grace helped Charlotte review the latest reports from both Pennsylvania and Virginia. Although both colonies had quite a bit of farmland, Pennsylvania also had factories to produce parts for automatons, tools, and even mass produced carriages.

"Have you noticed that none of the colonies with sizable slave populations have factories?" Charlotte murmured. "All their finance is dependent upon farming, which means upon the vagaries of the weather."

Grace nodded. "The northern colonies have been much quicker to embrace automatons because they are cheaper than a servant. A slave, though, is cheaper still if you just keep breeding your own."

Charlotte looked up at her with her mouth slightly open, and then closed it with a snap. "Grace Elizabeth Fitz George, the only thing more offensive than the way you just phrased that is the fact that you are perfectly right. It's rather that colonies, like Virginia, are trapped, wealth bound up in slaves and not in advancing into the future."

She had a thoughtful look that made Grace instinctively nervous, but she knew better than to pry or distract. After a bit, she returned to going over the reports, releasing Grace with a smile when it was time for her visit.

"Have fun for me," she murmured.

"Be wise and calm for England," Grace whispered back. "And, if all else fails, off with their heads."

The snort of laughter followed her out of the room.

****

Grace had offered to bring Susan with her, which was completely out of her way but also extended her escape. She was glad she had when the girl was handed up beside her, almost bubbling with excitement.

"It's not that meeting Her Majesty wasn't incredible, but imagine, a woman who still runs a business after she's married! I find that so inspiring. Mother supports Father in his work, of course, but it's his work. If I marry, I want to still be doing my own work."

Her own work, it turned out, was teaching music, which she already did at the tender age of sixteen. "I love teaching children. I don't think I could ever be truly happy if I wasn't doing that."

It made Grace feel a little old and woefully less sure of her future. Was there anything she was that passionate about?

I help Charlotte with her work. What would I choose on my own? Mr. Franklin's words came back to her, but she wasn't sure how exactly one decided what one wanted.

The roads were crowded, and the carriage slowed to a crawl, stopping in a knot of traffic. The usual chaos had apparently been magnified by a herd of cattle that had been spooked and had decided to run along the main road, instead of crossing it. Susan pointed out near misses and minor disasters with the enthusiasm of the young, and Grace sat back and enjoyed her commentary.

"Oh, there's Mr. Beauchamp! See, the gentleman who just rescued that woman's little dog." She waved excitedly out the window in a way no Londoner ever would have, sixteen or not.

Grace followed her pointing with an indulgent smile and blinked in something between surprise and consternation.

Mr. Beauchamp was her dockworker, in the guise he'd worn when he'd met and argued with Miss Farnsworth. His coat was well cut from a burgundy colored cloth, his cravat was impeccable, and he wore a simple but expensive looking ring on one hand. He also smiled at Susan with every appearance of avuncular affection.

"What are you doing out and about on this fine day?" he asked her teasingly as he approached the carriage. He paused just a moment at the sight of Grace and smiled again. "And will you introduce me to your companion?"

Susan laughed. "Lady Grace, may I present Monsieur Pierre Beauchamp, one of my father's students. Mr. Beauchamp, will you be reading any of your poetry tomorrow night?"

Grace put out one hand quite correctly. "Charmed, I'm sure, Mr. Beauchamp. Are you a poet then, or do you study for the ministry?"

Pierre—she doubted it was his real name, but it was as good a way as any of referring to him—gave her a look of rueful amusement.

"I dabble at poetry and have no calling for the church. The good reverend has been teaching me philosophy and history." There was no hint of a French accent. If anything, he sounded more British than American.

"Please, good sir, why don't you join us?" Grace offered, prompted by some demon she rarely let free. "My coachman can drop you off wherever you like when Miss Paul and I reach our destination."

Pierre looked at her sharply, but only nodded. "That is very gracious of you, Lady Grace." He opened the door and swung himself up across from them, his back to the horses, and the door clicked into place behind him.

"And are you from Boston originally?" she asked. She was quite certain that none of the answers would be completely true, but she was curious about what story he had concocted, apparently for some time.

"Not originally, no. I was born in Maine. It wasn't officially a colony yet, of course. I grew up in both Maine and Quebec," he answered easily. "I came to Boston to further my education, both at Harvard and privately."

And just what private lessons taught you how to climb into upper story windows, eliminate killer automatons, and handle a ship like a sailor? "And what did you study at Harvard?" she asked aloud.

"The usual fare, physics, philosophy, navigation, literature, alchemy and airships." He lifted a hand in dismissal. "Reverend Paul is kind enough to say I have an ear for discourse, which is to say that I have no more useful skills."

This was so preposterous that she had to frown not to laugh. "And how did you come to be the reverend's student?" She didn't say, she didn't have to, that a white man choosing a black reverend as his mentor with all the hordes of scholars available was *unusual*. The only thing more influential on social standing than breeding was money, and by strict definitions, the reverend and his family had neither.

"I heard him speak," Pierre said simply. "When you have, you'll understand."

Susan beamed at the praise of her father, and Grace only nodded.

"Then I will look forward to it."

They spoke of more general things for the rest of the trip—the city, the turning colors of the trees, the poetry reading the following night, and the poets that could be expected to attend. Maria Gowen Brooks had promised to attend, as had Lydia Childe, already published at the age of twenty-three, and the black playwright William Henry Brown. There were more that Grace had never heard of.

"Will Master Edgar be there?" Pierre asked.

Susan frowned. "He should not. His family would not approve, and if one is to defy one's family, one should also be prepared for all the consequences that may come. I do not approve of people breaking rules in secret, trying to have both freedom from tradition and freedom from responsibility for their actions."

Grace tilted her head in unspoken inquiry.

Pierre explained, "He is from Richmond, where the traditions of segregation are more weighty," he said delicately. "The Poe family is wealthy, and for their son to visit with white abolitionists while here would be a minor scandal. I've no doubt that they would view the reverend's social evenings of mixed races, poetry, and politics as the work of at least minor devils, if not Lucifer himself."

Susan scowled fiercely. "That is why Boston is considered the Athens of the Americas. We are not perfect, certainly we have far to go, but besides the Philistines of Virginia we are as close to a shining city on a hill as the early founders could ever have wished or expected."

"I look forward to getting to know more of the city, and know that Cha—that Her Majesty will be grieved that she is not able to attend." Grace frowned. "I wonder . . . if a more private gathering could be arranged for her at the governor's mansion? Perhaps a dozen people, on an afternoon, to give her some taste of what she is missing?"

Susan nodded. "It would be good for her to better know the people she rules."

Pierre smiled. "One could not argue with such a sentiment. However, I believe we have arrived, and I must bid you fair ladies farewell."

He handed them down, waving off the footman, and refused Grace's renewed offer that he make use of the carriage. "It is a fine day for a walk, and I haven't far to go."

It *was* a fine day, sunny and almost warm, and the elm trees that lined the street were brilliantly yellow. For a moment, Grace allowed herself the fantasy of being able to walk down the street beside him, merely enjoying the day. *And would that be a better, or a lesser memory than that kiss would have been?*

Being both expected and known, they were greeted far more eagerly than Mrs. Hanover and her companion had been. Verity barely let the butler announce them, and they shed last names and titles with their wraps.

"I'm so glad you've come! I know I should offer you refreshments first, but I absolutely cannot wait to show you my newest model. Do you mind terribly?"

Grace laughed and Susan twirled around in excitement.

"Please, show us at once!" the young girl sang. "I have never met a woman inventor before, and it makes me feel . . . . Oh, truly feel that anything is now possible!"

Verity led them at a walk that just barely didn't turn into a run. "Now, it is rather an odd idea, or at least to my knowledge no one has tried it before, but it seems so eminently sensible to me. . ." She broke off and flung open the door to the back room.

Technically, the room was almost certainly a ballroom, and a large one at that. It had been taken over entirely with worktables, crates of supplies, and automatons in various states of crafting. In front of them, however, was a bronze dog the size and build of a Rottweiler, complete with docked tail and ears. It wagged its tail at their approach, almost as if it were alive.

"Meet Rufus. He can fetch any article he is familiar with—glasses, knitting, a cane—can herd and supervise small children as well as animals, can run faster than a man, acts as a body guard when necessary, and can swim for up to twenty minutes without damage to himself."

Susan clapped her hands with delight while Grace studied the automaton more closely.

"However did you fit that much mental capacity and a power source in such a compact design?"

Verity spread her hands modestly. "It's true that the more things an automaton is trained to do, the more room you need for the central processor. I've been experimenting with peripheral nodes of consciousness, all connected to the main processor. There are nodes around the gears in all four limbs, as well as in the head besides the ocular and olfactory sensors."

They admired Rufus and watched as he was set through his paces, recognizing not only Verity's misplaced glasses, but also the book she had been reading earlier in the day. Finally, they sat down to tea, a substantial meal that could have replaced both lunch and dinner as far as Grace was concerned, with only a little room left for a late supper.

"How did you talk your husband into letting you continue your business?" Susan asked.

Verity laughed. "It was my main condition before agreeing to marry him. It's actually my uncle's business, originally, but it works better for me to take over the designing and leave him to the selling. With help, of course. He's fairly absent minded when it comes to money and organization."

Susan nodded. "Papa is the most brilliant man, and can keep track of a dozen things in his head . . . as long as none of them pertain to the daily bills. I wonder if this is a general failing in men?"

Grace, who had had to fire two tutors who had believed the female brain was unsuited for mathematics, coughed and reached for her tea. "Probably not in all men. People are people, and some are better at different things."

The conversation drifted to music, art, and poetry, with a smattering of steam technology and politics. By the time the tea tray was removed, Grace felt that her mind was as comfortably full as her body. *I need more women friends. With Evelyn dead, there's really only Charlotte left at home.*

Grace waited until Susan was off using the necessary to bring out the spider automaton. Verity was entranced and immediately started taking it apart.

"This is ingenious! Poison, enough for several dozen bites, by the look of things. Almost certainly something lethal. Enough power to last for several hours, heat seeking and attracted to motion . . . . I mean, it's horrific, but brilliant."

"How much do you think they cost?"

Verity frowned. "Likely, several thousand pounds for one, and I doubt there would be much of a discount for volume, given the complexity. May I keep this?"

"As long as you promise not to make more, certainly you may." Somewhere in the neighborhood of a hundred thousand pounds had been spent for a single assassination attempt. There was serious money afoot.

Susan returned, and they reluctantly took their leave of one another with promises to meet the following night.

"But there will be men there, and there never seems to be as much sensible talk when men are present," Susan lamented.

Grace choked and Verity coughed, but both agreed that it was sadly true.

Chapter Eight

Charlotte summoned her the moment she returned to the house. She was in her dressing room with two of the seamstresses and held up a dress to Grace as she walked in.

"Hold this against your skin. Let me see how it looks."

Grace held it up obediently. "It's not my usual style."

"It's not for you." Charlotte repeated the ritual with five more dresses, then, nodded. "Take these six with you, and make whatever alterations you need to in the ones they choose," she instructed the seamstresses. "I trust I will receive your very best work, as always."

Grace looked after them, perplexed. "Charlotte, what are you up to?"

"I'm going to invite the Pauls to the ball."

Grace grimaced. "Are you sure that that's . . . kind?"

Charlotte sighed and sat down heavily on a brocaded chair. "I can't afford to be kind. There are one and a half million African slaves in the fifteen colonies, and they are my responsibility. I can't change things in big ways without also changing the social barriers behind them." She shook her head. "The Pauls are educators, upper-middle class, and would be considered acceptable to attend if they were white. I can't leave that unchallenged."

Grace picked up a discarded gown and hung it in the wardrobe. "I'm sorry. I suspect that the Pauls will be willing participants, but I'm sorry you have to decide based on the big picture rather than on people. And I do understand, Charlotte. I'm just glad I'm not the one who has to do it."

Charlotte laughed with a tiny hint of bitterness. "I worry about my children. Raising them up to care and still be able to do this. . . . I'm not sure how to go about it. My uncles, even my father, God rest him, never learned it. Of all the sacrifices a ruler must make, I think the sacrifice of one's children is the hardest."

Grace bit her lip. *And if I have children, what kind of life will they lead?*

****

The thought recurred, inevitably, at the poetry reading the next night. Mr. Twilight was there, tan and handsome, as mixed race as she. There were a dozen young black men his age, and half a dozen young white men, not counting a bevy of teenagers, who seemed too young to have an interest in poetry.

Of course, Mr. Beauchamp—Pierre, whose name was likely a lie—was there as well. Chairs were gathered into a circle with one after another rising from their place to read or recite. Much of the poetry was very good, but she would have paid more attention if he hadn't chosen to sit next to her.

Well, perhaps if he hadn't come at all.

His voice was a rich baritone, and when he read, she felt as though something in her was melting. There were many fine voices, male and female, so she couldn't pretend that it was merely his voice. There were men just as handsome, some of them single. There were even other men present, who smelled pleasantly of soap. It wasn't any of those things, or even all of them. It was simply him.

Reverend Paul gave an introduction to one of the reader's, the black playwright William Henry Brown. It was simple, but heartfelt. Even in that brevity, Grace obtained a glimpse of what drew people to the reverend, and why people of different races and classes would gather in his home with every sign of eagerness and comfort.

After the readings were over, there were refreshments, and the group broke up to gather into small knots of conversations. Pierre steered her towards the refreshment table, and then back to join Verity, who was in an animated conversation with Lydia Childe, the poet.

"I think perhaps we should talk," he murmured softly.

"Yes, we should," Grace murmured back more bluntly. "Are you going to sneak into my room again, or shall we meet a trifle more conventionally?"

He gave a snort of laughter that made Verity look up, smiling, and Grace performed the introductions reflexively. Mrs. Childe was pleasant, but reserved, while Verity looked sincerely interested to meet him.

"If you didn't bring a carriage, sir, perhaps we could give you a ride home."

To Grace's surprise, he agreed. To her deeper surprise, Verity had the carriage take her home before dropping off her guests.

As she stepped out of the carriage at her own home, she whispered to Grace, "You can thank me later."

Grace felt herself blush, grateful that both the darkness and her skin color hid it. Pierre cleared his throat as the carriage started into motion again.

"I think your friend suspects a romance."

"It is very kind of her and suits our purposes. I take it that you have something more to tell me, or do you just want to make sure that I don't destroy your current cover?"

He winced with one hand over his heart. "You wound me, mademoiselle. Monsieur Beauchamp is as real as Lady Grace. That doesn't mean that there isn't more to both of us."

She shook her head, smiling despite herself. "Have you news on any other attacks on Her Majesty?" she persisted.

"Rumors more than news. It looks as if the volunteers outside the governor's mansion will become an official undertaking while your queen is present. So that is one piece of good news. But she is still in danger, and that means that you are as well."

Grace brushed that aside. "The Empire can survive without me. It won't be nearly as good a place without her."

He smiled. "Your queen is lucky to inspire such devotion."

It clicked, suddenly—the wilds of Maine, the French he spoke as a native. "Your queen is Marie Antoinette, isn't she?"

"While I live," he replied, the smile suddenly stilled.

They were getting closer to the governor's mansion, and she threw the dice of her emotions. "May I kiss you?"

"Mademoiselle?"

"I'll take that as a yes." She pulled his head down to hers and kissed him thoroughly, enjoying the catch in his breathing that matched her own. He kissed her back hungrily, but he never put his arms around her, and when she stopped, she saw that both his hands were clenched on the seat beside him. His eyes were very bright.

"You play with fire, mademoiselle."

"I'm not playing."

It wasn't strictly true, as they both knew that the carriage was pulling up to the governor's mansion even as she spoke, but it allowed her to exit the carriage with dignity intact and feeling somewhat in control of the situation.

"Adieu, mademoiselle," he murmured after her. "Pleasant dreams."

Dreams of the long awaited kiss would certainly be sweeter than of murderous spiders and cloaked assassins. She was just a little worried that she had miscalculated.

She wasn't forgetting that kiss any time soon.

Chapter Nine

Grace had been attending balls since her coming out at age seventeen. Thanks to her parentage, there was no place in London society where she was considered an interloper.

That was not to say that it had always been easy or pleasant.

America was oddly different. Parentage still mattered, but what one had done with that parentage was considered almost as important. Self-taught people of modest wealth were considered socially on par with people who had inherited the same. A famous name was an opportunity, not a guarantee.

Going over the list of guests with Charlotte, Grace felt almost dizzy. There were very rich and prominent abolitionists, professors, successful business owners, and farmers. The Pauls and the playwright she had met at their poetry reading were the only colored people invited. *Besides me, of course.* Four or five out of five hundred was barely a symbol, but it would most certainly be noticed.

The upheaval, as usual, started long before she and Charlotte even awakened in the morning. Although the ballroom had been scrubbed and polished all week, it had to be freshly cleaned and inspected for the smallest imperfection that day. Tables were brought down from the attics, and chairs were taken from their storage areas in lesser rooms. When they came down to breakfast, it was to find that every servant in the house had been roped in. So the butler, looking slightly put upon, brought them their food and tea.

"Should I offer to help?" Grace asked diffidently as they ate an unusually quiet breakfast.

Charlotte laughed. "Only if you want half of them to faint and the other half to feel offended that you didn't trust them to manage things. This is a day when we are better off quietly in our rooms writing letters until we have to submit to getting ready."

Charlotte, of course, had a great deal of letters to write. Dozens of official ones, and her usual daily letters home—one to her husband, and one to each of her children, even the baby. Grace obediently wrote a pleasant and innocuous letter to her father, who would likely only remember where she was when he read it. She would have written Great Aunt Elizabeth, but that would have jeopardized the queen's ruse. Instead, she stared out the window, looking for anything interesting.

Or for a particular blond Frenchman.

That kiss had almost certainly been a tactical error, and one she would definitely repeat at her first opportunity.

She wandered down to the kitchen to collect their lunch tray and spare a maid from having to bring it up, hoping to take Joshua back up with her to practice his letters. He, however, was polishing silver with an air of great excitement and privilege, so she was left to go back upstairs with only the luncheon tray to keep her company while Charlotte was busy with her correspondence. For a house with near a hundred people in it, the mansion felt like an incredibly lonely place.

The local volunteers guarding the queen had of course been augmented by replacement troops sent on the next airship. The British troops were better dressed and more orderly, but there seemed to be some fraternization going on between the two. Looking out at them, Grace had the odd feeling that she was caged, trapped there, however well meaning her jailers.

It was a relief when Milly came in to dress her hair. Charlotte was wearing red and gold, a reminder of her rank, and Grace was in midnight blue with silver. The flowers Milly had decided on were white with blue throats, stark against the darkness of her hair. Once she was dressed, she had to admit that she was in her best looks.

A pity the only one likely to notice is the governor, and he isn't likely to look above my cleavage.

Charlotte had not given in to the temptation to make a late entry, but at least her status meant that she didn't have to wait in the receiving line. She was given the finest chair in the room, grand enough to have been considered a throne in some countries, with courtiers to wait with her for those deemed worthy to be brought up to be introduced.

Grace was not so fortunate. Standing next to the governor, whose eyes strayed to her bosom whenever there was no one else young and female to ogle, she greeted the first guests to arrive. It was a relief that Verity and her husband were early, so she had at least one friendly pair of faces among the curious.

"We should talk, if there's a moment," Verity murmured as they nodded to each other, and Grace smiled back.

"We'll find one, certainly. After the third dance, seek the retiring room." The whispered aside made her feel as if she might actually enjoy the evening.

The Pauls were visible in line, Susan's face alight with excitement and nerves. Grace smiled reassuringly before turning her attention to the portly man in front of her for the usual greeting.

"It seems that the queen's pet negroes are here. I wonder if there will be trained monkeys at supper?"

The voice was clear, slightly raised, and definitely meant to carry. Grace continued to smile at the man in front of her, although her gaze shifted long enough to identify the speaker, a middle-aged woman in expensive clothing a few people behind the Pauls. Grace saw the excitement dim in Susan's eyes before her back straightened slightly, her chin up and her smile set. Something like rage built in Grace, and she grasped the next guest's hand a trifle too firmly, causing the man to grimace slightly.

"So pleased you could come," she said, her expression bland. Two more meaningless greetings, and then the reverend and his wife, daughter, and protégé were in front of her.

"Reverend Paul! Forgive my rudeness, Governor Spencer, but Her Majesty specifically charged me to bring the reverend and his family to her as soon as they arrived."

The governor looked taken aback, but one did not question the whims of royalty. Smiling broadly, Grace ushered the four in, cutting through the crowds hoping for a moment of royal attention, and brought them up to Charlotte.

"Just as you requested, Your Majesty," she said, presenting them.

Charlotte, as far as Grace could remember, had been born quick on the uptake. She smiled graciously, even going so far as to take Mrs. Paul's hand and saying that she was sorry the lady had not been able to attend the dinner her husband and daughter had graced. "Next time, We hope to have your entire family in attendance."

She gestured to Verity and David, and quickly arranged first and supper dances for Susan and Mr. Twilight to be with these friendly faces. Only when Susan was led off by Verity, her smile restored, did she ask.

"What happened to upset you?"

Grace explained tersely, and Charlotte nodded. She summoned a footman, who brought the butler, to whom she gave calm and specific directions.

"You will find this woman. I do not care who she is, although that information may be useful in the future. You will tell her that her queen wishes to inform her that We take disrespect to one of our guests as disrespect to Ourself, and that since We have better manners than she has displayed, we will allow her to fabricate some emergency that calls her from this place rather than publicly throwing her out."

The butler took his instructions with complete equanimity. Throwing out potentially powerful guests was apparently less distressing that being called upon to serve at table.

When he had gone, Charlotte turned back to Grace and smiled. "There. Do you feel better? I know I do."

Grace nodded her head, smiling. "Thank you."

Charlotte quirked an eyebrow, then gestured for the line of guests to resume.

Grace considered returning to the receiving line, but there were limits to good manners. Instead, she went around the room as a surrogate hostess, making sure that young women had partners and that young men were not too shy to request dances. She allowed Mr. Franklin to sign her card for the first dance and David for the second.

The lines were finally slowing, and the musicians started to draw up their bows. The guests cleared the center of the room, and there was a long moment of hush before the governor walked to the queen, bowed low, and held out one hand. She took it regally and walked with him to the center of the ballroom, then held up her free hand, signaling the musicians.

Music filled the room, where silk flowers dotted with perfume reminded them of summer, despite the chill autumn outside. They danced alone for perhaps a minute before Charlotte raised her free hand again, signaling other pairs, who slowly joined in until the room was a swirl of color.

"You worry about her as though she were your child, and yet, I'd wager you're a few years younger," Mr. Franklin commented as he came to claim his dance.

Grace laughed shakily. "I hide it poorly, or you are too perceptive a man, Mr. Franklin. But, of course, I worry about her. She is England."

Mr. Franklin looked at her over his spectacles. "We say that about all our rulers, you know, but with her, it may actually be true. And England hasn't been blessed with many of her caliber. Henry the Second, perhaps. Elizabeth, probably, although she was a harsh ruler. So was Henry, come to think of it. Her father would have been a disaster."

"Mr. Franklin, there is a point where honesty comes perilously close to treason. Shall we enjoy our dance and avoid that?"

He barked a laugh, but turned the conversation to harmless things.

There was little break between the first and second dances, and so she had barely finished dancing with the inventor when David came to claim her. He looked foppish and harmless, but she could look past that to the intelligence in his gaze.

"I hear you approve of Verity's new project."

It took her a moment to remember the innocuous project of the automaton dog rather than his wife's investigation into the nature of the spider assassin devices. "Rufus is amazing. I think it is a brilliant idea."

"Everything she does is brilliant," he said and smiled. "I'm sorry, the besotted husband makes for a poor dance partner."

"Not at all. I can think of no one more deserving. And she does rather feel the same way about you."

His smile was blinding enough that she could see how Verity had fallen.

They chatted amiably about Verity's virtues, the automaton business, and the cost of heating a massive ballroom that was used perhaps four times per year.

Grace was sorry when the quarter hour and the song were over.

She was turning to go back to Charlotte when a voice stopped her.

"May I hope that you have saved me a dance, mademoiselle?"

He was dressed as Pierre again, a trifle finer than the previous evening, but a perfect upper-middle class or midlevel gentry figure.

She could not help but smile. "Monsieur, I happen to know that you were not on the invitation list."

He smiled back. "A friend brought me in place of her son who was indisposed."

She quirked an eyebrow. "Did you bribe him or blackmail him?"

He took her hand. "Mademoiselle, you wound me. He was delighted to play cards with friends this evening, so, in fact, neither bribe nor blackmail was necessary. If anything, he feels that he owes me a favor."

She laughed, unable to help herself. "You may have the supper dance and the last dance. And, if you behave yourself, you may walk with me to the refreshment table and carry some lemonade for me as if I were too fragile a feminine flower to possibly do so for myself."

He looked down his nose at her. "But, of course, mademoiselle."

They walked sedately, her hand on his arm, smiling at the people around them. "Just how many people do you lie to on a daily basis?" she asked pleasantly.

His tone was light when he answered. "Mademoiselle, I have never lied to you. Not once. That I am cautious with my truth is not the same thing as falsehood."

She let that percolate a few moments. "You seem genuinely fond of the Pauls. I believe, perhaps foolishly, that you wish the queen, my queen, safe."

He was silent a long moment. "We all balance what we love. I try my best to harm no one I care for, by action or inaction. I will not pretend that this is always an easy thing or that there may not be hard decisions to make."

That degree of honesty was unnerving, but they had reached the refreshment table, removing her need to reply. Only when he had found her a seat and offered her the promised glass did she ask the most important question. "Why are you really here tonight?"

"I am watching over the people I care about."

"You think there is danger here? Tonight?"

"Everywhere. Every night. But yes, I have concerns."

The musicians were finishing their own break, and she shook her head, frustrated at the lack of time. "Find Susan, would you? Dance with her if she doesn't have a partner yet. I'll see you for the supper dance in an hour."

His eyes laughed at her, although his face stayed calm and even. "I wouldn't miss it."

Someone approached to request the dance, and she turned to greet them. An hour, four dances, and then she could dance with Pierre once more.

It felt like an eternity.

It was fortunate that she had promised to meet Verity after the third dance. The ladies retiring room was set aside for quick repairs to dresses or hair, with a discrete entrance to the necessary room—which also gave it a discrete exit to the back of the house. It took only a few moments of idle conversation for the way to be clear, and Grace ushered her guest back to a small writing room that would have been used by Her Majesty's secretary if that gentleman had not perished aboard the airship.

"What did you find out?" she asked as soon as they were alone.

Verity pulled out her reticule and handed over a folded sheet of paper. "I analyzed the parts, workmanship, and modification against the life span of the central controller. Original construction is French, two to three years ago. Modifications are British, and based on the intricacy, I think we can narrow it down to these three suppliers. Final work was done about two weeks ago, which means either a master level engineer was present here in America, or the spiders came over on the airship immediately before or immediately after the one destroyed in the attempt on Her Majesty's life."

Grace blinked. "You can tell all that from a broken unit?"

Verity laughed. "Grace, this has been my life and my livelihood since I was fifteen. I could have made those modifications, but they would have looked very different. There are a half a dozen others in the colonies who also could have, but again it would have had entirely different signatures. I don't know how many masters each of those three establishments has, but it brings it down to no more than a dozen people."

Looking over the paper, Grace shook her head. "Verity, you are amazing. If only Evelyn—" She stopped, the loss painfully new again. "A friend of mine who was perfect to check this out in England was on the airship."

Verity touched her hand. "I'm sorry. David and I can take a trip to England if Her Majesty needs us to. David still has family there, and we never did take a marriage journey."

"I'll let the queen know that you've offered. I hate to involve you in more danger."

"Have you seen my husband play the fop? No one will believe us anything but a besotted couple, and he can buy me something from every shop for me to compare. Besides, this is bigger than us. Charlotte, Her Majesty, is bigger than us. She's not just England, you know. She's America, too."

Grace hugged Verity. "Let's go back before I cry and need the retiring room in truth." She went to the door, opened it, and looked both ways, then turned back. "I'm so very glad to have you for a friend."

****

The supper dance was, traditionally, a waltz. Grace had become adept, over the years, at avoiding it with anyone she didn't already know and like. It was rather too close to public lovemaking to be enjoyable with lecherous older men like the governor. Or even lecherous young men because, much as they despised her birth, most of them would have taken her to bed as quickly as they'd have taken her father's money.

Standing up and going to Pierre, she felt a shiver go through her that had nothing to do with cold or uneasiness. He smiled slowly at her, and pulled her gently onto the dance floor. His hand sat at her waist, hers was on his shoulder, their free hands were clasped, and their bodies remained only inches apart so that she could feel the heat from him.

The musicians struck up again, and they began to move. She was aware of all the other couples on the dance floor, she had to be, not to hit one that misstepped, but it seemed she and Pierre were alone. She breathed in his scent—soap, leather, again that hint of pine—and sighed.

"This is the perfect time to ask you questions, and yet, I don't want to waste the dance."

He smiled. "A dance like this is part pleasure and part torture. And reminds me of the two other times I have had you this close."

She shook her head faintly. "I was sorry that I couldn't allow a kiss the first time, sorrier that it couldn't last longer the second time. But there are consequences, and I can't afford to forget them, for your sake as well as mine."

His grip on her tightened slightly. "Then we'll enjoy this sweet torture to the fullest, shall we?"

The basic waltz was easy to learn, easy to follow. Susan, she could see from the corner of her eye, was doing fine with David, while Verity contrived to make it look as if Mr. Twilight was leading. All around them, couples were doing the same dance, tamely.

Grace had danced with extremely talented partners before, had seen what the waltz could be turned into, so it wasn't a complete shock when Pierre turned movement into magic—into a twirling, sweeping tide. She had never danced like that with a man she desired before. It was precisely a sweet torture. One she wanted never to end and suspected would kill her if it didn't.

She didn't notice the couples around them drawing away, many of them stopping. Only when the music ended and the clapping began did she realized that she had been the focus of attention. It was a dubious thing for a royal bastard to be, and her eyes turned instinctively to find Charlotte. The queen was smiling and clapping with the others, and Grace took a small sigh of relief.

Pierre was watching her, his expression a little closed. "Shall we?" he asked, holding out his arm, and she took it, allowing him to lead her into supper.

Chapter Ten

Supper was oddly comfortable. It was easy to see how much arranging Charlotte had done. The Reverend and Mrs. Paul were seated some distance away from their daughter and protégé, with a table of abolitionists and clergy. Susan and Mr. Twilight were seated diagonally from each other, emphasizing the mixing of black and white. American dignitaries were seated with British poets, and all the easy little groups that formed and persisted so easily in society were broken up, mixed into the greater whole.

Pierre appeared to have noticed as well. "A cunning and wise woman, your queen," he murmured as he brought her a plate of food. "I'm surprised she didn't include red Indians in the mix."

Grace shook her head. "She won't dilute her message, even when there are other things she wants to change. She learned, before she was even queen, to fight your battles one at a time, not all at once. And sometimes settle for a gain you can actually get, rather than your whole goal. It's hard, but that's part of what it means to be queen."

Mr. Franklin and a few others joined them at the table then and talk became general. Pierre was already acquainted with Mr. Franklin and, apparently, had some connection with the gentleman's deceased mother. The two spent the rest of supper largely topping each other's humorous anecdotes, which left Grace feeling both amused and a little cheated. They had one more dance together, but it wasn't a waltz.

Still, she was in a fairly good mood when she returned to the ballroom. However, she soured faintly when she saw who Pierre was leading out in the next dance. Miss Farnsworth was lovely in pale blue, her pale blond hair going nicely with his, a few shades darker.

If Miss Farnsworth was guilty of treason, it shed doubt on Pierre's innocence. But looking at them dancing together, Grace admitted that the predominant emotion she felt was not suspicion—but jealousy. She tried to shut that out and focus on suspicion, which at least was rational.

Miss Farnsworth's mother was French. Were there actually relatives still in France to be bargained for? Or had Napoleon offered a return of old estates in return for spying? He'd used both blackmail and bribery in the past, and Heaven's knew that France would be happier with England in disarray from the loss of her queen.

Grace danced with her partners, kept up polite conversations, and kept an eye on both her French suspects. It was, as Great Aunt Elizabeth had once commented, rather like playing chess when one or more of the pieces had been replaced with scorpions.

Three dances later, she saw Pierre grow still in the middle of the dance floor. It was a subtle thing, as he never stopped either dancing or conversing, but she noted the tension in him. Miss Farnsworth, dancing with Mr. Twilight—and she had no doubt that Charlotte had arranged that—did not seem to notice. Grace smiled and danced, and at the end of the dance thanked her partner and strode off purposefully—not to where Pierre was, but to where his attention had been drawn.

It was cold outside, but, with the heat of the assembled guests, the doors to the garden were still slightly ajar. Grace slipped through the narrow opening in time to see Pierre tackle a small figure.

Grace had learned a trick as a small child, setting each foot down toes first to avoid the sound of dislodging stones. She moved as silently as a woman in a full ball gown could, but she knew Pierre was aware of her presence as she reached him. His captive was a street urchin, not much older than Joshua.

"What was he doing?" she asked softly as the child started and wriggled to look at her.

"A bomb. And I suspect that he is actually a she."

The child cringed and then stuck out his or her chin. "Ain't doin' no harm. Brought a present for the lady in red and gold, supposed to hide it under her chair to surprise her."

"And how much did they give you to do it? A shilling?"

The child swallowed. "A guinea."

Grace shook her head and picked up the child. "Don't struggle, because I don't want to have to hurt you. Didn't anyone ever warn you that if you're offered that much money, you're likely to end up dead?"

The child, amazingly, did not struggle. Pierre was looking over the 'present', a red and gold knickknack the size of a child's ball.

"Can you disarm it?" she asked. "Is there a timer or some other activator?"

"A timer, I think. And the safest thing to do with it is to put it into the pond, where the shrapnel will be slowed by water." He carried it carefully and set it down beside the scenic pool before using a fallen branch to probe the water. "At least six feet deep, so that should do to prevent any significant damage. We still should move back from here."

"And what do we do with the child? If we let her go, they'll certainly track her down and kill her." Grace sighed. "Charlotte is going to insist on keeping her. Do you know what it's like living with a queen who persists in adopting stray children?"

Pierre laughed, a baritone sound that reached to her toes. "Actually, yes, I do. There are worse things."

The child's eyes had grown bigger as they talked, and she suddenly began to struggle. "Don't want to be kept in a cage by a queen!"

Grace shook her briefly by her collar. "It's not a cage. It's a house. And I think we'd better have her meet you."

Sneaking back into the mansion was slightly harder with the child, so they compromised on Pierre taking the waif in through a window, while Grace went in through the door she had exited. She went to the nearest footman and murmured a message to him for the queen.

"Please inform Her Majesty that Lady Grace says that Mr. Thompson's papers are available for her perusal." Then she walked around the room's perimeter to the door to the retiring room, and exited.

Pierre was waiting in the writing room and had managed to produce an apple to feed the child, who sat on the floor devouring it as if it was the first food she had had all day.

It probably is.

"Did you learn anything more?" she asked, playing with the reticule that hung from her right wrist.

Pierre shook his head. "I thought she'd have a better memory if she was less hungry."

Grace surveyed the child before sinking down into a chair and setting her reticule on her lap. "What made you realize she was a girl?"

Pierre shrugged. "Practice. A lot of street children dress as boys. They're more likely to get jobs and less likely to be swept up into brothels."

"Surely not at such a young an age . . ."

Grace's protest died at the gentle shake of his head, and she swallowed, feeling ill. A soft sound caused her to stand, her hand closing around the small purse as the door opened and Charlotte slipped in.

"Your Majesty."

Pierre bowed, and the child stopped eating the apple to stare. Charlotte was as majestic as she had appeared in the ballroom, perhaps more so in the smaller, plainer writing room. The gold and red of her gown matched the coronet of yellow and crimson rosebuds in her brown hair, and she looked serene, but very much in charge.

"What have you found, Grace?" she asked quietly, her eyes on the child.

Grace kept her own eyes on Pierre, the gun now out of her purse and hidden in the folds of her dress. *Trust is all well and good, but there are limits.*

"This child was paid a guinea to hide a present under your chair. The present was actually a bomb, which is currently at the bottom of the gazing pool."

"Likely set for midnight, when you would be there to give your toast," Pierre interjected.

Charlotte looked down at the child. "What is your name, child?"

"Em-emma," the girl stuttered.

"And do you know who I am?"

"You're Charlotte Augusta, Queen of Britain, Canada, Australia, India and America," the child breathed. "I didn't know, ma'am, really I didn't. I wouldn't be blowing up anybody, 'specially not *you*."

Charlotte sighed. "Do you have family?"

Emma shook her head.

"Then I suppose you'd best stay and be a sister to Joshua. What can you tell me of the people who hired you?"

It had been in the morning. There had been a woman, wrapped up in veils, and two men. Grace kept the gun ready while Charlotte skillfully interrogated the child about details—the carriage, the clothing worn by the men, details of fashion and demeanor. They had told her how to get around the guards, how to get inside the building. She was supposed to act when the company was at supper, but had been slowed by a trysting couple in the garden that she couldn't sneak around.

Pierre interjected questions when she described the watch fob on one man, asking about the horses, the waistcoat, and the shoes. It was amazing how much the child remembered, but Grace reminded herself what she had had to learn to recognize by this age.

Pierre was clearly agitated by something, but Charlotte remained serene.

"Grace, would you fetch Mrs. Potter, please?"
"Charlotte, I don't think—"
"Grace."

The tone was gentle but implacable, and Grace sighed. "Fine. Then you can hold onto this while I'm gone." She angled her body between Pierre and Charlotte as she handed over the gun.

Pierre raised an eyebrow. "I am wounded that you do not trust me, mademoiselle."

He sounded cheerful rather than wounded, and Grace smiled.

"I do trust you, monsieur. I might very well trust you with my life. But I do not trust you with the heart of England. I barely trust myself enough for that."

Charlotte rolled her eyes but kept the gun trained on the Frenchman. "Hurry along with you, then. You know how I hate these things."

Grace managed not to laugh as she closed the door behind herself.

Finding Mrs. Potter was the work of only a few minutes, and she was not at all surprised when Charlotte turned Emma over with firm instructions to feed her, bathe her, and find her a bed. Pierre was nowhere in sight for that interview, but reappeared as soon as Mrs. Potter and Emma were gone. Charlotte removed the gun from her pocket and handed it back to Grace.

"There. Now, what did you learn, Monsieur Beauchamp?"

Pierre looked grim. "I believe I know one of the men involved. He's in Maine. He has ties to France but has always maintained that his allegiance was to the old monarchy and not to the Corsican. I find that now suspect."

Charlotte nodded serenely. "And what do you intend to do?"

"I intend to go to Maine and find out what I can."

"Then I'm going with you," Grace interjected. "It will only take me a few minutes to pack."

Pierre turned to her as if to protest, but Charlotte raised one hand. "Yes, I think that is for the best. We can let it be known that Great Aunt Elizabeth has taken a turn, and you have gone to her. Mr. Beauchamp was gracious enough to drive you to the train station."

Pierre looked as if he was going to argue but nodded. "Pack lightly and less obtrusively if possible."

Grace snorted, turning for the door. Behind her, she heard Charlotte serenely continuing. "We trust not only that you will return this cousin to Us safely, but that you will also give Our regards to Our royal cousin in Her exile."

There was a slight choking noise from Pierre, but Grace was already headed for the back stairs.

Servant stairs were a terrible waste of space, but wonderfully convenient for getting around unseen. She raced upstairs, pulled the flowers from her hair, and shed the dress with a muttered apology to Milly, who would have to deal with the mess. She changed into a black walking dress and a hat with a veil, and shoved her plainest clothing into a valise. She was running back down the stairs again in somewhat less than ten minutes.

Pierre was still there, waiting, Charlotte watching him with that same regal serenity that meant she wasn't going to back down.

"Excellent," the queen said. "You'll need money. Here, take this. Now I need to arrange a prolonged volley of shots at midnight to hide the explosion from the gazing pool." She shook her head a little. "I won't say to stay out of trouble, but try to control collateral damage."

Grace embraced her, slipping the note from Verity into Charlotte's hand. There was no change at all in the queen's expression as she nodded her head to Pierre before returning to the ballroom.

"Are you going to keep a gun trained on me all the way to Maine?" Pierre inquired politely.

Grace grinned. "Probably not." The gun was in her jacket pocket, which was easier to reach than the valise. "Shall we?"

They reached the front door easily enough by avoiding the ballroom altogether. A few early retirees were already leaving, but the line to retrieve carriages was not terribly lengthy. Before long, they were directed to a light racing carriage behind a pair of matched bays, and Pierre handed her up to the single seat before climbing up beside her.

"We should be able to get eight hours out of these horses before they need to rest. It's unlikely we'll be able to change them on the north road, so we'll have to break about dawn. We may make it to Amesbury, but no further, I don't think. It may be wiser to take a room for the night sooner, but we'll see how the road and the horses hold up."

He hadn't mentioned how they—how she—would hold up for hours in an open carriage on a chill night. However, he pulled a large wool blanket up and over the two of them from behind the seat.

It was cold, and the gaslights of the town wouldn't follow them far. Still, the moon was nearing full, and the road as the town fell away not as rough as she had feared. The racing curricle was going at a great clip—at least five miles per hour, perhaps even faster. Soon, the city lights were dim behind them, with only occasional lights showing in windows they passed by.

Pierre did not talk at first, concentrating on the horses and the road, and Grace was willing to share his silence. The valise she kept between her feet to avoid losing it over bumps, and she confirmed that the gun was safe in her pocket before giving in to the comfort of leaning against him. After a few minutes, he adjusted the reins so that one arm was around her, and they continued on into the night.

"How many days are we going to be on the road?" she asked eventually.

"Four, if all goes well," he replied.

"Ah. This might be a good time to ask, then, if you would like to share my bed during this adventure."

There was a moment of silence, and then he laughed, tightening his arm around her. "I was not intending to take advantage."

She snuggled closer under the blanket. "You're not. I'm asking. You are free to decline if you prefer."

He growled a curse she wasn't familiar with in French. "You will almost certainly be the death of me. And I'm not at all certain that I'll make it to Amesbury with that kind of temptation swaying me."

She smiled to herself and closed her eyes.

She did not, strictly speaking, sleep. She opened her eyes at each town, most dark and shuttered, and was aware when the moon set as the false dawn lit the sky to their right. She straightened up as the horses slowed and smiled up at Pierre.

"Amesbury?"

"Amesbury. There's an inn here, and if we are lucky, they'll be willing to put up both us and the horses for a few hours. If not, Salisbury is another half hour." He hesitated a moment. "I'll be introducing you as my wife, of course."

She blinked. "Is that legal in Massachusetts?"

He shook his head. "This far into the country, they'll care much more about an unmarried woman traveling with a man than the shade of either of our skin."

She shook her head but lowered her veil without further comment. It didn't take much acting to look tired and frail when he helped her down, and she listened without comment to his tale of family illness and a rapid trip to a deathbed in the wilds of Maine. An exchange of coins, and the innkeeper's wife was leading them to a room while an ostler took charge of the horses.

A fire was hastily laid in the room, and a maid showed up with a basin of hot water. "Would you want food now, or after you've had a bit of rest?"

"Later," she murmured.

Pierre nodded. "We should try to get going again about noon, so if you could wake us for the midday meal, that would be perfect."

The maid and the innkeeper's wife both trooped out, and the door was closed and locked. Grace set down her hat and began unbuttoning her jacket.

"Grace, I know you're likely exhausted, and this may not be a good time to make this kind of decision," Pierre told her.

She smiled as she pulled off her jacket and began unbuttoning the black walking dress.

"Are you always this noble? Or are you that exhausted yourself?" She took a step closer, smiling up at him. "Or are you just not interested?"

He groaned before pulling her into his arms. "I am trying to be noble."

The kiss was better than the one in the carriage had been, because he wasn't holding back. *Was it really only a day and a half before?* There was an urgency that she reveled in before pulling back.

"Help me with my buttons?"

His fingers fumbled with the first one, but he repeated the maneuver with growing certainty until the gown slipped loose from her shoulders. Her breath caught as the fabric fell down to reveal the thin shift that was all she wore.

It was cool in the room, despite the fire, but she didn't care. She stepped out of the dress and put it carefully over a chair before turning back to Pierre and untying his neck cloth. He shrugged out of his jacket, and she turned her attention to the buttons on his white linen shirt. His skin beneath it was smooth and warm with a tiny area of golden hair on his chest.

"Grace, before we go any further . . . Are you sure?"

Grace snorted. "I am very much the instigator here, if you hadn't noticed. I'm not a child and not a virgin. I have had several . . . . Well, two . . . well planned affairs with men who were in a position neither to be punished if caught nor to be forced to marry me. This is not nearly that deliberate, and I will admit to being overwhelmingly attracted to you, but that doesn't mean that I don't know what I'm doing. And speaking of before things go any further . . ." She reached into her valise and pulled out one of the sponges and the flask of wine she had hastily packed. "There are far worse things than being a royal bastard, but I'll do my best not to create another."

Pierre laughed. "Mademoiselle, you are a wonder. And we will make sure to take advantage of those things at the proper time. But for now, kiss me."

She moved back into his arms, raised her face to his, and purred as he pulled the pins from her hair. His mouth on hers was firm with the tiniest tang of salt, and his hands ran down over her body and through the thin fabric as though it wasn't there. *Which is an excellent idea.* She lowered her arms and shrugged off the shift so that it landed in a puddle at her feet, white against the dusk.

His breath came faster, and he pulled her back to him, burying his face in her dark hair and then kissing down along her neck. Lowering his head, he licked one nipple and then the other, and she felt her legs start to quiver.

I've done this before. I know what to expect. But she hadn't ever done this before, not like this, not with him.

She fumbled with his pants, not looking away from his face, and gave a sigh of contentment as they opened, and she felt the warm length of him under her hand. He started at the contact and raised his head from her breasts to fasten his mouth on hers again. She pushed his trousers down, still stroking him as he lifted each leg free.

"Bed," he said when he lifted his head again.

She nodded her agreement, laughing softly as he lifted her into his arms and took the three strides to the bed at a run. He set her down in the middle without letting go, and kissed her again as he lay down beside her.

"You are so beautiful," he breathed. He ran one hand lightly from her jaw line down her body to her hip.

She arched her back with a sigh. "Before we forget, can you grab the sponge and wine?"

He groaned, but pushed himself up, returning with it in a moment. Grace was careful not to spill extra wine on the blankets as she lightly soaked the sponge and inserted it. She had always done that part out of sight of her two previous lovers, but that seemed foolish now.

"Kiss me," she said, holding out her arms.

He slid back into them as though he belonged there. His mouth met hers, and her eyes closed in pure sensation. His skin was warm and smooth, except for a small scar on his right shoulder, and his hands on her body were deft and gentle. When he began to stroke along her thighs, she parted her legs, moving her hand to his erection.

"I'm not sure," he began, moving to still her hand.

She batted him away. "Hush," she said firmly, sitting up and pushing him back onto the bed. "I am." She climbed astride him, holding his gaze with her own as she gently angled him inside of herself. His eyes glazed slightly, and his breath caught as she thrust herself down onto him.

She laughed in sheer delight and grabbed hold of his shoulders as she thrust herself up and down. He growled something inarticulate, then he laughed too as he caught her hips and matched her, stroke for stroke.

"Oh, yes," she whispered, and then there was no more talk, just the rhythm of their bodies joining, and the music rising up inside of her until it was the only thing she could sense. She crescendoed, and he followed her a heartbeat later.

"Oh, yes," she whispered again, her lids heavy as she collapsed onto him.

He pulled the blankets up over them both, stilling her when she would have moved off him. It felt warm, safe, and wonderful, and within moments, she was asleep.

****

At some point during the morning, they rolled over onto their sides, but they were still entwined when the knock on their door woke them. Pierre kissed her before sliding out from under the covers.

He glanced over as he shrugged on his clothes. "How are you?"

She snorted. "Fine, thank you. How are you? I feel wonderful and like another twelve hours of sleep would be perfect." She grinned. "Maybe we can take a slightly longer stop tonight."

Pierre grinned back. "I'll check on the horses. We should get going as soon as we've eaten."

Grace lingered in the warmth of the bed for another minute after he was gone, then emerged and hastily put on her clothing. They were chilled, as was the room, despite the fire, but outside would be colder still.

I have absolutely no idea where this affair is headed. It should have been a sobering thought, but it made her smile instead.

Bringing little meant she had little to pack, so she was ready to go by the time the knock on the door came to signal that their food was ready. When Pierre returned, she was already half way through an immense piece of apple pie.

"Apple pie for breakfast or lunch. Is this an American thing?" she inquired.

He sat beside her on the bed and picked up another piece. "Pie is definitely an American thing. Pie for every meal, sometimes two or three kinds."

Grace looked at the remnants on her plate and shook her head. "Oh, to be able to eat more."

The day was bright, the sky a strange pale color with the sun giving light but almost no warmth. Grace was grateful to snuggle back under the heavy blanket as they set out again.

"Would you like me to drive for a while? I do know how."

Pierre looked at her and chuckled. "I'm waiting to find what you don't know how to do."

He handed the reins over, and she took them in her gloved hands, getting a feel for the horses through them. He wrapped an arm around her, but showed no signs of taking them back, and after a bit, she began to enjoy the experience. The roads were far less even than the ones she had driven most often in and around London, but she had seen some just as bad in the north of England.

"Do you expect the gentleman to be there, when we get where we're going?" she asked, her eyes on the road.

"I don't know. I expect we'll learn more about him, in any case, and I'll be able to warn those who need to know that he is not what he seems. He'll be dangerous, if we encounter him and he suspects that we know."

"A woman and two men. Any idea who the other man is?" She found herself wondering if the veiled woman was Miss Farnsworth.

Pierre shrugged, a Gallic gesture she felt rather than saw. "Not by Emma's description, but we'll need to keep our eyes open."

Having had carnal relations was not a reason to trust him, Grace reminded herself. "Do you think he's working for France, or for elements in Britain or the Colonies?" she asked, fighting the temptation to tell him what she knew of the spider assassins.

"It could be any, and I wouldn't be surprised if people from all three groups are involved in some capacity. It's a measure of how successful your queen is that so many want her out of the way."

Grace sighed. "The best ruler we've had in centuries, the most popularly beloved, and the most assassination attempts of any I've heard of." She shook her head. "You should try to sleep a little. I'll wake you if we come to a cross roads."

Pierre chuckled. "That will give me at least an hour. Nudge me if anything looks wrong, or if it starts to snow."

Grace slanted a look at him before returning her gaze to the road. "You don't look as if you're joking."

"Mademoiselle, no one from Maine jokes about snow." His arm squeezed her gently, and he settled against her much as she had him the night before.

Grace smiled to herself. Charlotte trusted her enough to sleep while she worked, but no one else ever had. It was a heady compliment.

Wanting you is dangerous. Liking you is more so. I truly don't dare to love you, my dockworker spy.

The roads in the north country of England might have been as rough, but they were rarely that desolate. The landlady had said that it was eight miles to the next village, but Grace hadn't expected that she would see nothing at all except fields and woods in that time. There were cart tracks here and there, and at one point, she saw smoke curling from a just visible chimney behind a hill. Otherwise, her only company was the man breathing steadily beside her.

She tried to imagine the isolation of living in that house, of never seeing another human being that didn't already live with you without extreme effort. Would it seem peaceful or horrifying?

She slowed the horses at a shadow on the road ahead, realizing that it was an entire flock of wild turkeys crossing the road in twos and threes. They were amazingly ugly creatures, ungainly and almost lurching as they walked, and she watched their progress with annoyance. They seemed to take no notice of the horses, and she pulled up with mild consternation to let them pass.

"How can anything that stupid survive?" she muttered. She'd tried turkey in England, and several times already in America, and she preferred chickens, thank you very much. Chickens got out of your way.

She started up the horses again as gently as she could, trying not to wake Pierre. The thud of their shod hooves on the packed ground was like a lullaby, but she wasn't in danger of falling asleep. The part of her body pressed against his was far too alert for that.

A sign in the middle of nowhere announced that they were in New Hampshire, and the road became noticeably rougher. She had a moment's uncertainty but tapped it down ruthlessly. Pierre hadn't mentioned crossing into New Hampshire, and her sense of geography was not sufficient to be certain that they should be, but there had been literally no place for them to turn off. Besides, people spoke of ships from New Hampshire, which meant it had to have a coastline. Most likely it was just between Massachusetts and the unknown wilds of Maine.

Her watch informed her that she had been driving perhaps an hour and a half when she encountered the first crossroad, with a weathered wooden sign indicating that the town of Seabrook was to their right.

She pulled the horses up and shook Pierre gently. "First Crossroads, as promised."

His eyes were somehow bluer than she remembered, and she caught her breath before laughing.

"What's funny, cherie?" Pierre stretched without taking his arm from around her.

"I am," she said, still smiling. "We're at the road for Seabrook, so I stopped to ask for directions."

"I see. The seagull over there probably wasn't very forthcoming with information."

It wasn't his eyes, it wasn't his smile. Perhaps it was the way he simply accepted that the world was a better place when one laughed at oneself. Whatever the reason, she felt her heart turn over. *Oh. That's it, then.*

He was smiling quizzically at her, and she started up the horses again. "So, still straight?"

"Still straight. Let me know if you tire and want me to take over."

Or maybe it's that he treats me like a person, instead of a delicate and brainless child. "I will. If you tell me what to do at the next towns, I won't have to wake you."

He shook his head. "I feel rested enough. We'll break at Portsmouth for supper if all goes well. Then, depending on the weather, perhaps go further."

He pointed out birds as they went, a fox off in the distance, and the ugly majesty of a moose on a hill. *Or maybe it's that he loves without apology. Because he loves this land.*

He paused, smiling that question again. "What's wrong, love?"

She smiled. "Nothing's wrong. There's just a lot to take in." *It isn't wrong that I fell in love with you. Foolish, certainly. Doomed, likely. But not at all wrong.*

She paused to ask him about a strange creature with a tail like a rat, and laughed at his preposterous tale that it slept by hanging from it during the day, and was usually only seen at night. Other than that, they kept on at a good clip, passing several more side roads and rarely a house or farm.

Evenings came deceptively quick. Grace prudently handed over the reins when the sunset turned the western sky to red. Within twenty minutes, it was full dark, with almost no light getting through the clouds from the shrouded moon.

"How far do you think we are from Portsmouth?" Grace asked.

Pierre shrugged, but he didn't appear to be smiling. "It should be only another mile or two, but it's going to take us a bit to get there." He pulled the horses to a stop and handed the reins to Grace. "I'll lead them with a lantern. Otherwise, we're likely to lose one to a broken leg."

Grace took control of the reins without comment. It wasn't as though there was anything to say.

The next hour felt endless as snow started to fall, and Pierre walked with the horses while she kept ready to pull them up if he stumbled. His lantern was only a halo of yellow in front of the horses, and she could only guess where the road was. The snow started to accumulate on the carriage sides and floor and frosted her head, shoulders, and lap.

When she saw the first light from the town, she thought she was imagining it, but a second soon joined it, and then a third. She got the impression of a bustling town, tiny beside Boston but far larger than Amesbury. Pierre signaled a stop, and she pulled the horses to in front of an inn.

"I think we'll spend the night here," he said cheerfully, and she laughed aloud at the relief.

Ostlers arrived to take the horses to the stables, and Pierre took her arm to lead her inside. The innkeeper directed them to his lady, a round white haired woman who promised them hot drinks, a hot meal, and a room.

It was heavenly just to be warm in a brightly lit place, and Grace felt almost giddy with it. "I really prefer traveling in daylight."

Pierre grinned. "I do as well, but there isn't a lot of that to go around this time of year. If the snow clears, we can leave at dawn, which will give us ten hours before dusk. That might get us to Portland, Maine if we're lucky."

Grace shrugged off her cloak, leaving on her veiled hat, and stripped off her gloves. She started with surprise as the returning landlady grabbed her left wrist.

"No wedding ring and a darky?" The woman's smile was gone. "I'll not have a darky floozy in my house, and shame on you, sir, for trying."

Grace felt something like hot ice flowing up into her as she held up her hand to stop Pierre's response. She stripped off her hat and regarded the woman coolly.

"Your prejudices and your provincial morals are of no interest to me. I am on a mission, and a look at the ring on my right hand would have told you from whom." She held out her right hand, the ring Charlotte had given her prominently on her middle finger, as that was the only one it would stay on.

"I have a writ in my purse that would have any subject of the Crown obligated to help me in any way possible without asking for payment. I also have guineas. Think about which you'd rather I produce, and then tell me, how much for your best available room?"

The older woman's face clenched, her lips flattened into a straight line. "Ten guineas," she said.

It was highway robbery, but Grace merely inclined her head. "Very well." She counted out the coins one at a time into the woman's hand. "As soon as we've finished our food and drink, you may show us to our room."

The food and drinks were already on the tray the woman had set down on her approach, which Grace thought was fortunate; no fear of anyone doing anything to it out of spite that way. She smiled pleasantly as the woman set out the food—beef stew, by the smell, and hot cider—and didn't let the expression fade until the woman had left the room.

"Do you really have such a writ in your reticule?" Pierre asked pleasantly.

Grace snorted. "Of course. I only bluff when there is absolutely no choice, and we still had several other options. A town this large would have had other inns."

He looked at her over his mug. "But you didn't want to seek out a friendlier one?"

Grace hesitated, taking a sip of her cider to cover it. It was stronger than she was used to with a pleasant warmth quite apart from its temperature. "To a small extent, I didn't want to let her win, and to a slightly larger extent, I didn't want to put the horses, or us, through another trip out tonight. But mostly . . . everyone has prejudices. It's important to upset them. The next time she is tempted to judge someone by skin color, clothing, or wedding ring, she may think twice. And that may be of help to someone else in the future."

He smiled at her so warmly that her traitorous heart seemed to skip several beats.

"You are an idealist, as well as a warrior. It's a good combination."

She felt her face grow warm and was grateful that it probably didn't show. "I suspect it takes one to know one."

To her delight, his blush was visible.

She kept the hat off—there was no point, now—and greeted the maid who came to show them up with a pleasant smile. There was a fire in the fireplace, and the maid placed warming pans between the sheets of the large canopied bed.

"I can have warm water brought up, if you like," the maid offered.

Grace nodded. "That would be lovely, thank you."

She sighed when the girl had left. "It's only six in the evening, and I'm ready for bed."

Pierre grinned. "I'm always ready for bed where you're concerned, mademoiselle."

She laughed at the outrageousness and moved forward to embrace him. "Thank you."

"For what?"

"Too many things to mention, and mostly just for being who you are. What you are. As you are."

He kissed her before taking a careful step back as the maid returned with the water. "I'll check on the horses and be right back."

She smiled again at the sweetness that would give her privacy for bathing after all they had shared, but it was nice to have a few moments alone. She washed herself as best she could from the basin, then, after a moment's hesitation, inserted a new sponge lightly soaked in wine.

In case.

She didn't expect to sleep when she'd only been awake six hours after the four hour or so nap in the morning, but she realized she had when Pierre slipped into bed beside her. Her hand uncurled from the gun under her pillow as she recognized him, and she put her arms around him.

"Should I let you sleep?" he asked softly.

"Mmm, no," she whispered back.

His mouth closed around hers. That morning, she had been the aggressor. Now, she was content to lie back, to let his hands wander over her, his mouth move from hers to her neck and breasts. When he entered her, slow and smooth as silk, she sighed with pleasure and just a hint of sorrow.

So this is making love.

She was young to know for certain, but she didn't think there was going to be a fourth affair in her life. This one was spoiling her for anything else.

Chapter Eleven

They left just before dawn. The snow made everything surprisingly bright after the storm had blown through, and Grace was happy to find that Pierre's racing carriage converted into a sleigh with very little work. After tips to the ostlers and the sleepy maid, they were on their way.

They crossed over into Maine perhaps a half hour later, but with the snow-covered roads, it was impossible to tell if there was a similar change in conditions. Kittery was a tiny town that was behind them almost before she had time to register. After that, there were more and more woodlands, with fewer clearings and no farms close to the road. The trees on their right were noticeably more bent from the sea, and it made Grace realize how exposed the road truly was.

Pierre drove, as Grace had little experience with sleighs.

"I've only really felt snow a dozen times in my life," she explained as the horses took off, seemingly undisturbed by the few inches of snow they strode through. "It sometimes snows in January, but the only time I saw snow in November or December was 1816."

Pierre snorted. "November? In '16, we had snow every month of the year in Maine, including July. All the crops froze except the potatoes, and wolves were taking down livestock inside pastures."

Grace sighed. "We thought it was the end of the world, the weather was so bad that year, and then

Charlotte was so sick with her first. We thought, if she dies, that's just it. Everything will end. But she lived, and she had little George, and she convinced everyone that failed crops couldn't stand in the way of English ingenuity. And I still had my coming out that year. I was seventeen. Everything was silk flowers because Charlotte convinced everyone that it was their patriotic duty to grow food instead of flowers in the hot houses."

Pierre laughed. "I just can't imagine you in one of those court dresses, all in white, ostrich feathers in your hair."

She tilted her head to see his profile better. "You sound as if you've witnessed a presentation to the queen before."

He smiled but did not answer, which made her remember his promise that he hadn't lied to her. It was slight confirmation, but left her oddly satisfied. For some reason, he didn't feel he could tell her how he knew so much, but he wasn't lying about it. That counted for something.

They talked about music and taught each other a handful of silly songs from their respective homelands. Some of Pierre's were French, other's American, and she wondered again how he could turn his accent on and off like a gaslight.

"Were you born in Maine?" she asked.

"Yes," he replied. "We're heading to the town where I was born, Belfast. It's a smaller town, not much bigger than Kittery."

Grace frowned. "That's an Irish name."

Pierre nodded. "Most of the people are from Ireland, or at least their parents or grandparents were. Probably a hundred or so are from France originally."

"Like your parents?"

He paused. "My father died before I was born. But my mother was from France, yes."

Again, she had the sense of truths withheld, but she could live with that. It reinforced his statement that he at least wasn't telling her anything untrue.

And how many people in my life can say that? Even Charlotte would lie to me if it was for the good of England.

They paused for lunch and to rest the horses in Biddeford, a mill town, apparently, reinventing itself now that steam technology was replacing water wheels. Grain and lumber mills still ran from the nearby waterfalls, while steamwork facilities were developing for plows and other small machines.

"The ground is too rough for most of the automatons you use in England," Pierre informed her. "Perhaps someday things will be that tame here, but I hope not."

A cluster of natives was present outside one of the stores they passed, and Grace had to clench her hands not to point. "Red Indians are present in the towns?"

Pierre nodded. "Some live in the towns, although those usually adopt European dress and manners. But many come in to trade, and they adopt any technology they happen to admire, ignoring the rest. They are changing as much with the steam technology as we are, but very differently. We use automatons to churn butter, they use steam vents to dry their fish for winter."

The snow was the perfect depth for fast travel—enough to make the sleigh glide smoothly, but not enough to tire the horses. By the time the first stars came out, they had made it to the outskirts of Portland, a bustling seaport about the size of Portsmouth.

"Fifty miles in a day on New England roads. Is that some kind of record?" Grace teased. Pierre laughed.

"It would have taken longer without the snow, and if we'd had a heavy snowfall, we wouldn't have gotten half this far. But no, good horses make a great many things possible."

Grace debated internally whether she was going to try to hide her race at the inn there, and in the end, opted to let any fallout be immediate. She removed her hat with its veil and strode in with her head held high, and her hand on Pierre's arm. His eyes smiled, as if aware of what she was doing, but he made no comment.

The landlady was a young slip of a woman, her apron failing to hide an obvious pregnancy, and she looked no more than politely interested in their arrival. "How many rooms will you be wanting?"

"One," Grace replied firmly before Pierre could answer. "And would it be possible to arrange a bath?"

"I'm afraid it will cost extra," the landlady apologized. "And it will take about an hour to arrange. Would you like a meal in the main room while you wait?"

The main room clearly doubled as a local tavern, as there were a good two dozen people in it, most of them men. The tables and benches were polished oak, and firelight from the fireplace sent shadows around the room that the gaslights couldn't quite dispel. It was warm, cozy, and surprisingly friendly.

The barkeep directed them to a small table off to one side and brought them two tankards of hot cider without being asked. From the clothes of those assembled, it looked like a gathering of farmers, crafters, and machinists, although there seemed no division among the groups. A single black man sat among the others with no obvious sign of isolation.

"I tell you, I was there," one of the men was saying, his voice mellowed from alcohol but not yet drunk. "The angels must have saved her, there's no other way to explain it. This explosion ripped the sky, and then the airship came raining down in pieces, so you couldn't even make out whole bodies. There were some parts, though, I heard later. And there she was when the smoke cleared, her white dress scorched and marked with soot, but not a mark on her skin."

"I think it was Parliament that set her up to die, the right bastards," a more belligerent voice opined. "She's our queen, and England's, but those blokes hate her like the plague."

"I say it was the Frenchies," another disagreed. "Napoleon probably wants to get her out of the way, so he can take Quebec back over."

"What about the South? Those colonies are plumb crazy."

Pierre quirked an eyebrow at her, and Grace fought not to laugh.

"She's very beloved," he murmured.

"She cares, and she's not afraid to show it. That's a rare thing in anyone, but especially in a ruler."

"It's not always enough to make a ruler loved back. I think Parliament is so universally hated that it makes her more lovable."

The landlady arrived with heaping plates of chicken pie, sliced ham, potatoes and boiled greens. It was more food than Grace usually ate in a day, and she stared at it in mild dismay for a minute.

"No one goes hungry in Maine, I see."

"Hospitality is considered a matter of honor," Pierre agreed. "Even if a family is short themselves, they'll make sure guests have more than enough to eat."

Even in the dire year of 1816, Grace had never gone hungry. It was distressing to think how often that was untrue of others, although it was clear that the inn had little to worry about.

"To Queen Charlotte," she said, raising her tankard to Pierre's.

"To Queen Charlotte," he replied, and others nearby took up the toast.

It made the cozy room feel even warmer, and Grace smiled as she started in on her food.

When they had finished, it was still only six in the evening, and Pierre requested that they be awakened at three and that a basket of food be packed for them.

"It's a good hundred miles to Belfast," he explained in an aside to Grace. "If we leave before sunrise and stop after sunset, we may be able to reach it in two more days. Any delay at all, and it will take three." The set to his face when he said that implied that he felt they needed to get there as soon as possible.

As they went up to their room after, Grace mused on how fast they had settled into something like routine on the journey. She had never slept with a lover before, and it was surprisingly intimate. *It's going to be hard, when this is over. How strange to be grateful for slow travel and bad roads because it prolongs this.*

The room was smaller than the previous night, but cozy with a stone fireplace and a black fur rug in front of the fire that appeared to be a bearskin. An oak table held a white ceramic pitcher in a bowl, while a chest at the foot of the bed served as a good resting place for their two bags. A picture of a ship at sea completed the décor, a reminder that no place there was far from the ocean.

There was a hipbath ready in the room, and Pierre again mentioned seeing to the horses. Grace turned, one hand on her hip, and frowned at him.

"It's not that you haven't seen me naked, and that I haven't seen you the same. It makes much more sense for you to scrub my back and then me to scrub yours, since we're going to end up in bed together anyway."

Pierre laughed, the low baritone tone that went to her toes. "I adore how direct you are. And, I will admit, that, most likely, the horses don't need seeing to. And I certainly don't want you to be in want of someone to scrub your back for you."

The water, when she ran her hand in it, was pleasantly warm, and there were kettles over the fire to add to it if it cooled. She started on the buttons at the back of her dress, but let her hands fall away as Pierre took over. He placed a kiss at the skin revealed, then continued down, a kiss after each button so that she was ready to forget the bath entirely by the time he slipped the dress from her shoulders.

"You are a dangerous man," she said as severely as she could, and he smiled.

"Mademoiselle, I was afraid you hadn't noticed."

She laughed as she slipped off her shift and small clothes and stood naked in front of him. "You'll want to take off your jacket, in case you get splashed."

He grinned as he set his jacket over a chair with her dress. "Are you inclined to splash in your bath?"

She smiled back. "You never know."

The water was wonderfully warm, and the room was pleasantly cool in comparison. The water covered her lower body with her torso and bent knees still exposed, and she handed him cloth and soap.

Pierre dipped the cloth into the water, rubbed it over the soap, and started washing her back. Grace would have sworn that there was nothing sensual about backs, but discovered that she would have been wrong. Her eyes closed, and she found herself purring as he massaged her neck, back, and shoulders. When his hands slipped around to her breasts, she caught her breath and leaned back, the lazy swirl of warm wet cloth over her skin hypnotizing as he went lower still.

"Do you want to wash your hair?" he asked. "There's a pitcher, so it would be easy enough to manage."

She weighed the benefits of clean hair, with no way of knowing when they'd next have the chance, against the harms of waiting longer to make love to him, and ruefully agreed. She angled her body forward so that her chest was against her knees, with her head back, he gently poured the warm water over her hair.

"I've never felt hair like yours before," he said. "It feels like lamb's wool when it's wet, soft and springy."

"My mother's, I'm told, had much tighter of a curl and was jet black," Grace told him drowsily. "She was a wonderful dancer, one of the best of her generation, but it was how she carried herself that attracted my father to her. He told me once that she moved more like a princess than any royalty he'd ever met."

His hands massaged her scalp, but he didn't answer immediately. After a few moments, he rinsed her hair and handed her a small towel to blot it dry.

"It's hard to miss something you've never had, and yet we do, don't we?"

His blue eyes were sympathetic, and she swallowed, feeling surprisingly close to tears.

She shook off the feeling, standing up and taking the larger towel he handed her. "Your turn, Monsieur, and you'll want your clothing off for that."

Wrapping the towel around herself, she stepped forward to unbutton his shirt, mimicking his style of leaving a kiss on the bare skin after each. It was warming to hear his breath catch, and her eyes were sparkling as she started on his trousers.

"Why don't we get me clean before you go any lower," he said in a choked voice.

She laughed as she let him go, and took one of the kettles from the fireplace to add to the water as he removed the rest of his clothing. Despite his protest, he still smelled faintly of soap, even before he lowered himself into the tub.

She washed his hair first, to give it time to dry, and to not detract from more pleasant activities. Then she took the cloth to his back and neck, and reached around to his chest. She let the towel fall from her body and pressed her naked breasts to his back as her hands went lower.

"You are most definitely both an angel and a demon," he said, catching her and pulling her into the tub and onto his lap. The water splashed a bit, but she just fit, and she laughed up at him until he lowered his mouth to hers.

The need was suddenly overpowering, and Grace turned her body until she was sitting astride him, her legs over the back of the bathtub. They were tantalizingly close there, and Pierre groaned before lifting her slightly up and onto him. Neither one could move effectively, but tiny flexes of his hips and clenching of her inner muscles were enough to drive each other insane.

"There is a perfectly good bed three feet from us," Pierre muttered, kissing her neck.

"We'd have to dry off first," Grace protested, wrapping her arms around his shoulders.

"That would take much too long," he agreed, and with another splash managed to stand in the tub, still holding her. She wrapped her legs around his waist, feeling him deeper inside of her, and held on as he stepped from the bath and laid them both down on the bearskin rug.

The firelight painted his skin in gold and orange, and droplets of water dotted each of them like liquid fire. The rug below her was as soft and smooth as silk, and as warm from the fire as the man above her was hot from more than the interrupted bath. He grinned fiercely at her, and she pulled his mouth down to hers before thrusting up with her hips to feel the entire length of him.

As though she had unleashed a dormant storm, he responded with a flurry of furious kisses while his body thrust relentlessly into hers. Her back arched as his mouth found one of her breasts and began sucking in time to his strokes. Warmth gathered inside of her, an ocean of heat, a well of emotion. She tightened her grip on his shoulders, head thrown back, feeling a scream of pure ecstasy building. She forgot her surroundings, forgot everything except the rising tide within.

It crescendoed, and she opened her mouth to scream, only to be met with his mouth on hers and the tide crashing over them both.

She must have slept, because she woke when he carried her to the bed and lifted her head drowsily for another kiss. He pulled the blankets up over them both and wrapped his arms around her. She listened to his breathing, and when it was even and still, she risked a whisper.

"I love you."

It felt good to have said it aloud, even though he couldn't hear it. Smiling, she slept.

Chapter Twelve

They rose before dawn and ate a cold breakfast with warm coffee to wash it down. Packing up the room was a matter of a few minutes, and Grace double-checked for her gun and her reticule before picking up the valise and heading out to the sleigh.

The inn was busy enough that there was someone awake to help them hitch up the horses, and, in minutes, they were on the road and had left the city behind.

There were no more cities after Portland. The larger road veered inland towards Lewiston and apparently took all the traffic with it, while they followed smaller roads closer to the coast. There was still enough snow to use the carriage as a sleigh, although the metal runners would occasionally clank against a rock poking through the snow cover.

"We got a good start again," Pierre commented. "We should be able to go as long as the horses can, anyway. They really need a good rest after twelve hours or so."

Grace nodded. "That's why the post coaches in England use automatons. They can go longer than the coachman and keep running all night in most places."

"The models for good roads are affordable, but something that would run here would cost a decent part of a king's ransom."

Grace remembered a few she had seen in London and nodded her agreement. "Not cost effective, so only the very rich would bother." She nodded to the flesh and blood horses in front of them. "Since we've another day at least on snow, will you teach me how to drive on it?"

Driving a sleigh was rather like skating while also controlling a team that turned much more narrowly than you did. Pierre was a patient teacher and did not even laugh the time she scraped a stone wall by turning the horses too abruptly.

"It just takes practice, like everything else. Waltzing, guns and diplomacy."

"And handling a ship's rigging?" she asked.

He grinned. "Lass, that's something I learned before any of the others. One does, growing up in a seaport, no matter how careful one's parents are. A ship comes in, and every eager boy, and a good number of the girls, run over to catch the ropes and tie her up."

Grace chuckled at the description. "I'd bet you were into everything as a child, and I'd bet that those big blue eyes got you out of it every time."

Pierre gave an exaggerated mournful look. "Ah, no, they did not, for my mother was wise and completely immune to my charms." They shared a laugh at that, and the topic shifted to small towns versus cities, and the charms of each.

Charm was not a word that Grace would have used to describe coastal Maine, although it had a stark beauty that reminded her of portraits of both the Swiss Alps and the Scottish moors in winter. All the trees they passed were evergreens, stunted and twisted by wind and weather in the open areas, and an impenetrable looking forest elsewhere. The wind was from the sea, raw and biting with the smell of salt, and sent the piled snow into odd sculptured drifts.

The clouds began to pull in around noon, and they took turns eating and driving, so as not to lose time by stopping. They hadn't seen a town bigger than three buildings since mid-morning, and Grace commented on it as she made herself a sandwich of sliced chicken and fresh bread from the seemingly inexhaustible basket.

"Was Falmouth the last fair-sized town until Belfast, or are there others on the way?"

Pierre guided the horses around a felled tree and glanced over at her. "Belfast is quite a bit smaller than Falmouth, but on this road it's the biggest town for a fair bit—maybe another hundred miles or two on up the coast."

Grace tried to absorb the distances involved and blanched. "Just how long is the coast line?"

"If you went from the start to the end overland, it would maybe be two hundred or two hundred and fifty miles. But, if you followed the coast the whole way up? No one's ever managed that, but I've heard guesses of over a thousand miles. One fellow I met swears it has to be over three thousand."

"I guess I'm glad we're only going to Belfast, then," Grace confessed. "Much as I enjoy your company, I don't want to still be doing this in January."

"January in Maine may be an acquired taste," Pierre agreed. "It's a good month to stay home by a warm fire and share good company, but not the ideal month for traveling."

Since Pierre was still driving, Grace allowed herself the brief fantasy of days in a snug house by a warm fire, with time enough to read, laugh, and argue, as well as make passionate love and fall into exhausted sleep. *Or simply washing dishes together.* She'd never actually washed a dish, but surely it couldn't be too hard to learn.

She took over the driving again for a bit, watching the clouds with growing concern. There was an almost purple darkness to them, and they seemed deeper than before.

"In England, clouds like that would mean rain," she commented carefully.

Pierre nodded. "In Maine, they would mean rain in summer. The rest of the year, they mean more snow."

And it was the part of the trip without handy cities to stop at. "So what's our plan for dealing with it?" she asked calmly.

Pierre shrugged, but his face looked worried when she glanced his way. "We keep going, because there's nowhere to stop here. It may not snow for hours, or it might even pass us by and snow somewhere else. And when the snow starts, we start looking for a place to hole up for the night. If worse comes to worse, the horses can keep moving all night, but they'll come up lame in the morning."

It wasn't much of a plan, but it would have to do. Charlotte was counting on them.

"You're worried about someone else besides Charlotte, aren't you?" she asked. "There's another reason you're in so much of a hurry to get to Belfast."

"When you find out that someone your family trusts is a traitor and a villain, it makes for some concern. If he'll sell out your queen, who else will he sell out? Friends? Family? His own queen?"

"Marie Antoinette," Grace said softly. "Your queen."

Pierre nodded. "I like and respect your queen, but my first loyalty has been to my own."

"You sound as if you know her," she pressed slightly, her eyes carefully on the road.

For a long moment, she thought he wouldn't answer, and then he sighed.

"You know how your Queen Charlotte adopts stray children? Queen Marie Antoinette has been doing so for quite a bit longer."

He didn't say anything more, and she let the implications of that wash over her. A man adopted by an exiled queen would have a more profound loyalty than any of those who freely accompanied her into exile. Especially Pierre. *Because when he makes a promise, I don't think he breaks it.*

The clouds darkened the afternoon, while the snow fought back by reflecting every tiny bit of light. Her watch said three in the afternoon when the snow began to fall, and she turned the reins back over to Pierre.

"Should we start to be on the lookout for a place to stop or wait?" she asked.

He barked a laugh. "We take the first place we find, since there hasn't been a single one in the past two hours. But we'll find something, and if we don't, we'll just keep going."

There was no argument with that, so she turned the topic to holidays, of which America had several and Britain had dozens. The snow brought her round to Christmas, even though she'd only seen a white Christmas once in her life.

"How do you celebrate here? The German style, the English, or something else altogether?"

"Most American's don't celebrate Christmas at all, except by going to church," Pierre told her, and then laughed at her horrified expression.

"No caroling? No wishing boughs, Yule logs, or plum pudding? No presents for the children?"

He shook his head. "Worse, no mistletoe for kissing the lad or lass of your fancy under. My family has a handful of small traditions, but mistletoe doesn't grow in America, and a fireplace big enough for a log to burn an entire week would let in more cold than it could ever hope to remove."

Grace folded her arms. "That just won't do. I'm going to teach you every carol I know, so at least one person will be able to go caroling with me come Christmas."

Neither of them mentioned that it was unlikely that she and Charlotte would be staying in America that long. Pierre cheerfully sang along with her as the snow continued to fall.

It was getting hard to see, and the horses were slowing in the increasing drifts when they saw the light. Grace had stubbornly continued through song after song as they progressed, to keep up both their spirits, but the relief she felt at the sight of that light told her just how worried she had been. Pierre turned the horses into the drive and up to the house only a short way from the road. A barn looked promising for sheltering the horses, and the house looked cheerful with the light coming out its four paned windows.

Pierre lifted her down from the carriage, and they walked together to the front door to knock. There was no immediate answer, and Pierre knocked again. There were voices from inside, and then the door flew open to reveal a teenage girl with a gun in her hands.

Pierre lifted his own hands slowly. "We're just travelers, caught in the storm, looking for a place to stay."

"You can't stay here," the girl said determinedly. "Ma is out at a birth and Pa is away, and I'm not to let anyone in. Not the queen herself."

"I understand," Pierre said gently, "but this is a dreadful storm, and there's a real risk of us freezing to death without shelter. We'd be happy to sleep on the floor."

The girl shook her head, her face set. "I'm sorry, sir and ma'am, and if it were only me, I'd take you in. I've got five little ones I'm responsible for, and I can't risk them to help the two of you."

Pierre looked ready to argue further, and Grace set her hand on his arm. "What about the barn? Could we and our horses shelter there? Maybe you could lend us a blanket or two? We'd be happy to pay you."

The girl looked uncertain, and Pierre smiled warmly. "That's an idea that doesn't make you break your promise, nor us freeze to death. I'd say your ma and pa would be satisfied with this. Even if there's livestock in the barn, it's not as though we could steal any in this weather."

The girl nodded warily. "Jeremy! Get me two . . . no, four of the spare blankets." She hesitated a moment. "And two pillows."

She asked them to back away when her brother, a boy of perhaps twelve, returned with the items, and allowed them to come to pick them up when he had moved away again. Grace left a guinea behind on the floor and nodded her thanks.

"Family always comes first," she told the girl. "I understand."

The barn was small, but well maintained, with chickens roosting in wooden boxes on one wall and two cows in stalls. There was enough room for the horses without the sleigh, but bales of hay took up the rest of the building, piled nearly to the ceiling. A hayloft above was half-full, and Pierre indicated it with a wave of his hand.

"I think that's our best bet. I'll hand up our bags to you."

Climbing the ladder was its own challenge in her traveling skirt, but she focused rung by rung, turning to take the bags when her shoulders were even with the hay strewn floor of the loft, and then reaching down again for the blankets and pillows.

"I believe we want a layer of hay down first, for insulation," Pierre advised as he climbed up after her. "Then one blanket down, us in all our clothes, and three blankets and the blanket from the carriage on top. If we're not warm enough with that, we can spread hay between the blankets."

"You believe. . . . So you haven't actually done this before, either?" Grace teased. "Still, that's more than I would have known, so by all means."

Three bales made a tolerably deep pile, and by the time they settled in, it was almost cozy.

"The pillows make everything better," she murmured as they curled against each other. "Straw is much too scratchy to lay your head on. I never understood how the baby Jesus was supposed to have done so."

Pierre chuckled, and she could feel the rumble of it. "Well, he was divine after all. Where as you are only half angelic, and I, not at all."

She wanted to remove her gloves to touch his face, but the cold dissuaded her. "My mother had the stage name of the Divine Night. That's the only claim to angelic nature I have." She sighed softly. "I don't even know her real name."

Pierre rubbed her back gently. "Names are not the most important thing. You know she loved you and wanted you to be happy, and that your father loved her enough to see to that for her."

She leaned up to kiss him, gently, on the mouth. "I have never known anyone like you."

"Ahh, love, I have never known anyone remotely like you."

There would be no need for the sponges. As much as she wanted him, and loved him, frostbite was a reasonable deterrent. Still, the overwhelming feeling she had was not lust. It was tenderness.

And there were only so many sponges, after all. Better to save them.

"Oh, sweet baby Jesus," she breathed.

"What's wrong?" Pierre asked.

"I forgot to use a sponge last night. I have never in my life been so careless."

Pierre stilled. "I forgot, too. And I usually have an excellent memory. I'm sorry, love. I know your feelings on royal bastards. I truly hope nothing has happened, but I have to admit, the thought of you having my child does things to me that I can't even explain."

Grace sighed. "In a different world, in different circumstances . . . yes. But we'll ford that stream if we come to it."

He chuckled again, pulling her closer. "That attitude is only one of the things I love best about you. We haven't frozen to death yet, we haven't been shot by an overprotective teenager, and we haven't failed in our quest. That'll be enough for today."

Chapter Thirteen

The chickens woke them before dawn, and Grace folded the blankets neatly before piling the pillows and another nine guineas on top.

"You are very free with your queen's money," Pierre commented, smiling.

"No, I used mine for this. She may have saved our lives, and almost certainly saved the horses, and she did the best she could with a hard decision. That deserves some recognition."

"Family comes first. What happens when someone marries into a new family?"

Grace snorted. "The families join, of course. Anything else would be foolish."

"You do realize that you've just called the last thousand years of European history foolishness, don't you?" Pierre asked.

"Can you disagree with that assessment?" Grace chided him. "Pride, power and money are terrible goals, if useful tools. Most of Europe has had that backwards since the Roman Empire."

There was six inches of snow inside the carriage, and between removing it and getting the horses back to the road, the first light of dawn was lighting the sky when they were finally on their way. Fortunately, the wind from the sea had left drifts along the inland side of the road, but the road itself was only three or four inches deep. After the rocky start, they made up considerable time on the way north.

"Not quite a five star experience," Pierre joked.

Grace glanced over at him, remembering waking up wrapped in his arms. "True, but the company made up for it." She opened up the basket of food. "Let's see what didn't freeze."

Cold apple pie with cheddar cheese was breakfast, and again, they traded off driving and fed each other bites as well.

"I think I have spent more time with you now than any other woman in my lifetime, except my mother," Pierre confided.

Grace snorted. "I've spent more time with you than any other man in my life, *including* my father. Royal dukes, as a rule, make terrible parents, although mine truly has done the best he could for who and what he is."

He was silent, and she remembered that he had grown up without a father.

"Explain Thanksgiving to me, again? I don't understand it," she asked, changing the subject. "It's because some of the early settlements didn't die out, while others did? How does that make sense? Why not just have royal proclamations of a day of thanksgiving when something good has actually happened, like in England?"

"The settlement in Plymouth and its survival are more an excuse than anything. Back in 1774, there was very nearly a rebellion in the colonies but cooler heads prevailed. Still, there were half a dozen incidents, any of which could have turned into full out war, and people were shaken.

"An infantry officer named George Washington proposed a yearly reminder of America's perseverance and survival, an annual day of thanksgiving to remember all that we have to be thankful for, so we always think hard before squandering it. Each of the colonies agreed to it in 1784, and we've celebrated it ever since." He winked at her and turned his attention back to the horses. "It's also an excuse to have entirely too much good food, and who can turn down that?"

She shook her head at him, happy to have provided a distraction. "As long as there aren't any songs about it."

"Of *course* there are songs about it! Americans can barely use a necessary room without writing a song about it."

She gurgled a laugh and set her mind to learning the first song.

A few strands of cloud hung far above them, but otherwise, the day was clear and bitingly cold. The temperature continued to fall as the day progressed, despite the sunshine, but at least there were no clouds threatening more snow. They reached the tiny town of Rockland a little before three, and Pierre slowed the horses.

"We can stop here, or we can press on for Belfast. It's about four more hours. It's clear enough that I don't think we'll have any trouble making it."

Grace considered the few buildings. "I'm guessing that they won't have an inn here, and you have family who can take us in when we get to Belfast?" At his nod, she lifted her hands. "Then let's go on. We've come this far, and I know you'll feel better when your warning is delivered."

His smile warmed her as much as the hot drink she fantasized over would have, and she smiled back, stamping her feet surreptitiously in her boots to keep them warm.

Her breath made a layer of frost on her veil, and her hands and feet were growing numb, but the horses were still moving strongly over the snow. She put her gloved hands under her arms for a few minutes until they tingled with painful warmth, and then held them out for the reins.

"Here, you need to warm your hands for a few minutes."

"Can I warm them on you?" he mock leered, but he handed over the reins and did as she said. After a few minutes, he sighed and nodded. "Good call. It's nice having a partner to watch your back."

Partner. She could not explain why the word gave her tingles, but it did. *The secret of a happy life is not wanting more than you can get,* she reminded herself. Her first governess had explained that to her, and she'd done her best not to forget.

The wind picked up after sundown, hurling ice crystals from trees and drifts into the air and at them. Grace was both grateful for her veil and worried about Pierre. The pale moonlight didn't show colors, but she suspected his face was far too pale. She warmed her hands as best she could for a few minutes before setting them on either side of his face.

"I would kiss you, but I think our lips would freeze together," he told her. "But don't give yourself frostbite."

"I won't. Just tell me when it starts to hurt."

In a few minutes, he grimaced, and she took her hands away to thaw them again. It was quite a bit longer before she took the right hand out again to cover his nose.

"No frostbite for your beautiful face. I forbid it. And we really need to get you a scarf."

"Madame ma Mere will be happy to oblige," he assured her, his voice muffled by her hand.

She switched to the left hand, when her right went numb, and kept that there until he confessed to pain from the returning blood flow. Grace fastened the large cloth napkin from the basket into a partial mask over his cheeks, nose, mouth, and chin.

"There, hopefully that will do it."

The moonlight was eerily beautiful over the brilliant snow and dark forests. A wolf howled in the distance, and she jumped involuntarily.

"They won't bother humans, and that one is miles away," Pierre reassured her. "They've mostly retreated to the interior, where the deer and moose still have herds. That's where most of the natives live, although new settlers encroach a little more every day."

Grace frowned, realizing that all her conceptions of natives were of people in warm places. "How do natives survive the winters?"

"They survive the same way we did last night, although they do have permanent homes and fires to help. Winter is only a problem if you're not prepared for it."

"Like bringing a scarf," she teased.

"Like bringing a scarf," he confirmed.

She snuggled close to him and looked up at the stars, brilliant in the sea of darkness above them. If she ignored having to stamp her feet to keep them from freezing, it would be an incredibly romantic moment.

"I'm a little sorry that the trip will be over," she sighed.

He didn't pretend to misunderstand. "We may have the trip back."

"We might," she agreed. "But regardless, I'm glad I came with you."

"I'll do my very best to not make you retract that in the days to come," he said solemnly. "And hopefully to have no more nights in haylofts, and no more guns pointed at you."

She laughed, the air sharp and sweet in her throat, and then there was a light visible on the road ahead.

"Is it too soon?" She checked her watch, but Pierre was grinning so that she could see it in his eyes above the ridiculous mask.

"No, we're home."

More lights appeared as they drew closer, and more, and then they were driving up to a large house with glass windows and a widow's walk. A boy ran out of the house to take the horses and shouted excitedly in French as Pierre lifted her down from the carriage and half carried her inside.

"I can walk!" she protested as she looked around. A stern faced butler stood at attention, while a petite white haired woman ran down the curved staircase toward them.

"Pierre!"

"Madame ma Mere," Pierre said formally, then spoiled it by picking her up and whirling her around before kissing her on both cheeks. "May I present Lady Grace FitzGeorge?"

The woman—truly, was this Marie Antoinette?—turned to her with a smile. "Welcome, my dear. Any friend of my son's is always a pleasure."

Grace curtsied carefully, wishing both that her feet had rather more feeling in them and that she knew what the protocol was for meeting a deposed queen in exile in the wilds of Maine. *When her adopted son is also your lover.*

"Thank you, Madame. I do not wish to intrude on a family moment, but I am grateful for your hospitality."

The queen snorted inelegantly. "You're not intruding. You brought my son back to me. But it's cold out, and you both look rather the worse for wear, so I'll send you to your rooms to recover and meet you for a late supper in an hour." She clapped her hands. "Bridget! Anton! Show them to rooms and bring them hot water to chase away the frost."

A few minutes later, a blithe Irish girl was taking off Grace's boots and exclaiming over her feet before submerging them in the agony of hot water. She then provided a shot of whiskey, which made the pain much more bearable, before starting on her hands.

"Your skin looks pale. 'Scuse me, miss, I haven't never seen frostbite in someone of your skin color, but I think we caught it in time." She pushed on a nail, released it, and seemed satisfied with the response. "There, a good warm soak in this basin, and they should be right as rain in Dublin."

The basin was on a wheeled cart that she brought over, so both Grace's hands and feet could enjoy the same torture that gradually began to feel almost pleasant.

"It's quite cold for November," the girl rattled on happily. "We usually get a good frost or two by now, and usually a few snows, but this is right cold. Cold enough to freeze the milk in a witch's teat,' my Daddy used to say. I expect he still does, but he went back to Dublin to see to some family business. We haven't seen him in a year, which is why I came to be in service to the Madame."

Bridget went through Grace's things while her feet and hands soaked, looking them over critically. "What you're wearing will do for now, but I'll get you a nightgown to borrow and wash all your things tonight. Looks like you've had a hard journey, but you'll feel better after supper, a hot bath, and bed."

"That sounds heavenly," Grace admitted. She wiggled her fingers and toes experimentally, pleased that all responded.

Bridget dried her hands, massaged lotion into them, and repeated the process with her feet. A whispered conversation with someone outside the door provided clean, dry stockings and shoes that were close enough to her size to be comfortable.

Bridget briskly fixed up her hair, looked at her a moment, and nodded. "You'll do."

Another servant was waiting outside the door to take her down to supper, so she didn't lose her way. The house was as large as many of the country estates she had visited, and she guessed there were probably two dozen rooms. The mixture of formality and spontaneity was charming, and the décor was just as whimsical, with classical pieces of art next to American pieces of recent decades.

The supper room held a table with chairs for eight and place settings for three. The queen was already present with Pierre beside her, and she rose to greet Grace.

"There, you look much more comfortable now. I won't keep you up too late, and a bath will be ready for you presently, but I do want to get to know you a little first."

"Did Pierre tell you...?" Grace asked hesitantly.

The queen nodded. "Yes, that an old friend of the family may not actually be our friend. We'll work on finding out more in the morning, and I have some ideas. It's a pity that the foolish rumor of my declining health caused the two of you to race up through such inclement weather, but I am of course delighted to see you." She frowned, her blue eyes shrewd but kind. "I think you had better be engaged, as people might be unkind otherwise."

"Oh, but—" Grace attempted but stumbled to a halt.

"My dear, you certainly don't have to marry each other if you don't both want to, but in society, strict honesty is not always the best policy."

There were too many convoluted thoughts, so Grace seized on the obvious. "Don't you have...concerns...about me marrying your adopted son?"

"You didn't think you owed him a kiss when he saved your life, you pulled a gun on him twice, and you left with him in the middle of the night without a chaperone to undertake a mad journey to bring warnings to someone you had never met. Frankly, my dear, I think you're perfect."

Grace sat back heavily in the chair. "I think I see where Pierre gets his view on the world."

"Thank you, my dear. You couldn't pay me a higher compliment." The queen beamed. "Now, let's get some food into you before you fall asleep unfed."

It was strange, after the long journey, to be served a salad course, a soup course, a fish course, and all the rest, just as if she were back at the governor's mansion. Well, not quite the same. The chef here was quite obviously French and excellent.

By the time she went upstairs, she was starting to weave a little, only partially from the wine served with dinner. Pierre stopped with her outside her door.

"Mother jumped the gun a little, but you should think about marrying me. After all, if we were married, you wouldn't have to take that bath all alone."

Grace smiled sadly. "I'm not sure if that's enough of a reason to marry. I've seen too many women married to men who regretted it after. Neither one is ever happy."

He shook his head slightly. "I wouldn't regret it." He kissed her and stepped back. "Good night."

"Good night."

As nice as the hot bath was, she couldn't stop thinking how much nicer it would have been if he'd been there, too.

Chapter Fourteen

A servant was on the lookout to lead Grace to the breakfast room the next morning. It was a bright, sunny room on the eastern side of the house, and the daffodil yellow wallpaper intensified the impression of light. A table with six chairs already held platters of food—eggs, sausage, toast, and the apple pie Grace was becoming used to for breakfast.

The queen was chipper in the morning. Looking at her, Grace wondered if she was ever not chipper. Her tendency to wave her hands around while she talked distracted her from eating, but there was nothing distracted about her sharp eyes.

"So, Monsieur le Serpent is up to trouble. First, we find out as much as possible about what he is up to. I considered a grand ball to introduce the two of you, for he would certainly come, but that brings him here, and not you there. I am sure that there is a good deal more to discover there. So we'll set out about eleven."

Grace blinked, not following her. "At eleven?" she echoed.

"*Bien sur*, to pay a morning visit on the snake and his wife. I should be able to convince them to host a dinner party in honor of your engagement, and that should provide plenty of time for my dear Pierre to snoop." She speared a slice of sausage and waved it for emphasis. "And when we know what he is up to, *voila*! We pounce."

Grace considered the state of her clothing and demurred. "I am confident I can pull off a morning visit, Your Majesty, but I didn't pack for dinner parties. Perhaps if you lured him away from home, so we could investigate that way?"

"Pray don't call me that. No one ever does unless I am in trouble." The queen's blue eyes sparkled, so much like her adopted son's. "Call me Madame if you feel formal and Mere Marie otherwise. As for the rest . . . no. In Paris, that would have been easy. In Maine, everyone notices everyone else, and the snow makes passage rather obvious. So I will get to have clothes made up for you and pretend that you will actually be my daughter-in-law. And if you change your mind and marry Pierre, so much the better!"

Grace choked and covered it with a sip of tea. "That's...very kind of you."

"No, it's not," Mere Marie replied frankly. "People think that I'm kind, and I do try to be, but generally, I just arrange things to suit myself. I enjoy people, and I like seeing them happy. So I help them for my own sake, quite as much as theirs."

Pierre shook his head and smiled. "And if all the world were selfish in such a way, the angels would confuse it for heaven."

Marie laughed lightly. "You are hardly an impartial judge, my dear. Now, after breakfast, we'll need to do some preliminary measurements on Grace, so that the seamstresses can start work while we are off on our morning diplomacy." She clapped her hands together like a child. "It will be so much fun! I will let the staff know now, so they will be available."

She ran off, her breakfast barely touched, and Grace stared after her, wondering if she was more amused or dismayed.

"She's—" Grace stopped, unable to think of anything both true and tactful.

"A force of nature," Pierre supplied helpfully. "Seven layers of fluff and silk over pure steel. Most people never look beyond the fluff."

Grace shook her head. "Pity the poor fools who make that mistake."

Pierre laughed. "She told me once that fittings for gowns were excellent practice in case one was ever in front of a firing squad, because if one can stand serenely for hours while one is jabbed with pins, the quarter hour waiting to be shot would be easy."

It was gallows humor, uncomfortably close to the truth, and very much what Grace herself had grown up with. "I like her."

"I'm glad. She likes you, too."

Grace cleared her throat, suddenly uncomfortable. "About that. Must we go on with a charade that we're engaged?"

Pierre nodded. "I told you that the far north is conservative. By bringing you to my mother's house I set that expectation."

"You might have warned me," she sighed. "I'm sure we could have figured out some way around it."

Pierre quirked a smile. "Yes, we could have hidden you in plain sight as an old woman, I suppose. But then we wouldn't have been able to share a room those three nights."

Her face grew warm, and she frowned at him before changing the subject.

The preliminary measurements involved only a half hour of standing and no pins. Bridget had done a good job freshening up her traveling dress and did her hair up for good measure. Before it was eleven, Grace found herself again in a sleigh with Pierre—but a larger sleigh, with a driver up front and them in the back with his mother between them.

"A beautiful day for a drive," Marie said cheerfully as they cut across fields. "I miss this, the six months it is too warm. Oh, sometimes we have enough snow in May or in October, but generally, this is something we only get to do November to April."

The thought that six months of winter could be considered too short left Grace with her mouth open and nothing at all to say. Pierre shared a look with her, his eyes dancing, and she closed her mouth and struggled not to laugh.

Monsieur le Serpent had been Viscount LaGrande before the revolution. He had fled the bloodshed after the king was executed, but before his estate had been confiscated, allowing him to bring a decent amount of his portable wealth with him. His house, some two miles outside of town, was more of an estate, with trees cleared back from the house in a generous radius. The house itself was stone and more ornate than any of the others in the area Grace had seen.

And isn't it strange how a tree lined drive is a mark of status in England, while cleared space means the same in Maine? It's all about what's hardest to attain and maintain, rather than any universal value of beauty or convenience.

A servant in what looked like livery ran out to take the horses, while their driver stepped down to hand Grace, Marie and Pierre out of the low sleigh. A butler already held the door open for them—*A shocking waste of heat*, Grace thought—and he closed it behind them as they entered the front hall.

While the queen's house had a central spiral staircase, the Viscount's took it a step further with galleries at the top for people to gaze down at new visitors. The room was done—overdone, in Grace's opinion—with a great deal of gilt and white marble, and a white marble fireplace against the walls on either side. These were indeed big enough for Yule logs and drafty so that there was a strong smell of smoke in the room.

"Madame!" said a man from the top of the stairs. "What a pleasant surprise!" He descended slowly, as if aware of his own importance, which gave Grace ample time to study him. He was of medium height and middle age, with thinning brown hair at the temples and a hint of stoutness. He also had a watch attached to a somewhat gaudy waistcoat, and as he neared them, Grace understood why the mention of it had fixed Pierre's attention. The watch was arranged so that a dragon appeared to be cradling it, with the head on top and the buttons the thing's eyes.

"Ah, Jules, my old, dear friend," Marie said with every appearance of warmth and sincerity.

Grace decided then and there not to play cards against her pretend mother-in-law to be.

"I have the greatest news, but you won't believe what prompted it. You know how people love to gossip…"

The queen's story continued as they were led into the morning room, an only slightly more muted room of pink and gilt. Servants brought tea and cakes, and Marie continued with her news. Full of details and references to mutual friends, she laid the framework of their story—a cold repeated as an illness, repeated as pneumonia, repeated as the entirely healthy Marie being on her death bed. So what should her beloved adopted son do but head out like a madman in the middle of the night to reach her in time.

"And if my dear Grace had not insisted on coming with him, who knows what trouble he would have found," Marie said fondly, patting Grace's arm. "But now he brings my future daughter-in-law to me with no warning for either of us! If I had known, I would have planned a dinner to celebrate their engagement. However, with so little warning and them needing to return to Boston as soon as the roads are clear again…" She raised her hands in a pretty show of helplessness while Grace concentrated on keeping a pleasantly neutral expression on her own face.

The lady of the house entered in at that point, smiling and gracious as though she had not had to dive into her clothes at a moment's notice, and the story had to be repeated. She was younger than her husband, and more tastefully dressed, with a pragmatic view on things that Grace rather liked.

"Well, all that truly matters is that they *did* arrive safely, you were *not* ill, and you have this happy news of an engagement to keep you warm through the cold months. Has a date been set yet?"

"Summer," Grace answered.

"The first of the new year," Pierre replied at the same moment. They turned to each other and laughed guiltily.

"I want a small wedding of just family, and not to wait," Pierre said smoothly. "Grace has family in England, and wants time for everyone to gather."

Madame La Grande smiled. "Well, you only marry once, so I can certainly understand that. Poor Jules had no family to come. Even if relations with France hadn't made it impossible, the rest had all perished."

A fleeting expression on the Viscount's face convinced Grace that there were further details to that story, and that she would far rather face the Viscount over cards than either his Lady or Mere Marie. Madame La Grande was forceful enough to have been the veiled woman Emma had described, and seemed brighter than her rather vain husband.

"This is such a lovely house, you must hate to leave it," she offered. "And quite the distance from Boston. Have you visited?"

"Oh, certainly, in summer," Madame La Grande replied. "Jules goes often enough on Business, and just returned a few days ago before the snow. Now, though, I'm sure he won't be leaving again until at least April, barring emergency. We both dislike travel in winter."

Grace shuddered theatrically and smiled. "I can't imagine why!"

The others laughed politely, and then Madame La Grande leaned forward to pat Marie's hand. "My dear Madame, you must allow me to give a dinner party to introduce your daughter-in-law to be to the community. Shall we say day after tomorrow?"

"Oh, I couldn't possibly," Marie demurred.

Grace caught Pierre's eye to share in her amusement. He smiled slowly at her, and for a breathless moment, she forgot where she was.

"Then are we agreed?" Madame La Grande was saying,

Grace blinked, wondering what she had missed. The viscountess was looking from her to Pierre and smiling.

"Ah, it is good to see young people so in love."

Grace felt her face warm and hoped that her skin color hid the blush. Marie laughed in delight.

"Oh, it certainly is. Pierre, why don't you bring Grace back to the house while Helena and I work up a guest list and write the invitations? I don't think she's fully recovered from the rigors of the journey." Marie turned to the Viscount with a smile. "Poor Jules, I am stealing still more of your wife's time"

"At least I know it is in a good cause," he returned with a gallant little bow.

Grace and Pierre rose obediently and made their goodbyes as a servant was sent for the sleigh. The coachman looked cheerful and warm, and Grace guessed that he had spent the visit in the warmth of the kitchen, possibly flirting with some young woman of the house.

"I *am* still tired," she confessed as Pierre handed her back up into the sleigh. "Next time, we should try to keep our adventures down to just two or three days."

"I'll make a note," he promised gravely.

She laughed aloud.

"It would be much more convenient to adventure together if we were married," he teased gently, his voice too low to be overheard by the coachman up front.

Grace studied her gloved hands, unwilling to say no and unable to say yes.

There was a moment's silence before Pierre cleared his throat. "If our…impetuousness…has consequences, you really need to, Grace. Both of us grew up without a father, and I want better than that for any child of ours."

That brought her perilously close to tears, and she closed her eyes without answering. They travelled in silence the half hour back to his mother's house, and he helped her out of the carriage before asking one of the servants to bring her tea in her room.

"Rest well," he said gently, for once without the slightest hint in voice or expression that beds had better uses than sleeping.

She nodded, not trusting herself to speak, and went upstairs.

Chapter Fifteen

The French community in Belfast was small and tightly knit, perhaps a hundred people in fifteen extended families. Representatives from each of the families had to be included, not to slight anyone, and Marie returned in time for the evening meal brimming with success.

"So, the Viscount was absent from home on the day he was presumably seen in Boston," Marie summarized as they sat down to a dinner of poached salmon, potatoes and seafood chowder. They were less formal tonight, with no distinct courses, and Grace was feeling a little better after a good cry and a short nap.

"Can anyone corroborate that his Viscountess was at home as she said?" Grace asked.

Marie nodded. "Yes, she was seen by several people during the days her husband was gone."

"So she's not the woman under the veil." Grace nodded. "Any idea who the second man might be?"

Pierre shook his head. "No one from home during that time fits the description, so I don't think he's from here. It appears to be a true conspiracy, rather than a few disgruntled people acting on impulse."

"Conspiracies abound," Marie commented sadly. "It is ever that way when one is royalty. If they don't want to kill you, they want to use you, and frankly, I find the assassins less wearisome than the toadies."

Pierre's eyes grew hard, and Grace wondered what he was remembering. A servant came in to clear the table, and they spoke of the weather, and the upcoming party, until they were alone again.

After the meal, Marie excused herself with a smile, leaving Grace and Pierre alone together.

"I think your mother enjoys matchmaking," Grace said as lightly as she could. "I met a Mr. Franklin who says she is the reason he was born on the right side of the blanket."

Pierre shrugged. "It's a French trait, and although she wasn't born French, she has it in full measure."

He was close enough across the table that she could have reached out to touch his hand. "The spiders we fought in my bedroom—did someone release some here?"

He nodded soberly. "We lost three people that night, and were very lucky not to lose more. After that, my brother and sisters were sent elsewhere, to hide under new names in different places."

"But not you."

He grinned. "There are definite advantages in not being in line for a contested throne. I, and two of my sisters, were considered safe. They've both since married and gone about their lives. I'm the youngest of the family, the last to grow up, and the only one my mother has currently under her roof."

Grace thought about little George, Elizabeth, and William growing up in the shadow of the throne, and she nodded. "I have been grateful on occasion not to be legitimate. I don't want to be a playing piece in the royal game of marriage chess."

He winced at the description and nodded. "And does that have you opposed to marriage in general?"

She sighed. "Pierre, if I hadn't come on this trip with you, hadn't been compromised by rural standards and perhaps impregnated, you would never have thought of marrying me. That's a terrible foundation for a lifetime."

"I'm not sure you're right about that. Very few women have ever pointed a gun at me once, let alone twice, and the kiss in that closed carriage was something to remember. But I think a better question is, if there were no pressure, no worries about opinion, morals, or a child, and no risk of sudden death, would you have any interest in marrying me?"

He rose so smoothly from his chair that she was not at all prepared when he crossed to her and lowered his mouth to hers.

"Just to remind you of the possible benefits," he whispered huskily when he let her go. "Now, I think I'll go throw myself into a snow bank before I ignite."

She laughed, but she also stayed sitting for a few moments after he had left to make sure her legs would carry her.

They had never put it into words, but she knew they both felt that sneaking into one another's bedrooms would be an abuse of their hostess's hospitality. It made things easier, especially with not increasing the risk from the one unprotected night they'd already shared, and she respected him and herself more for it.

However, in moments like that kiss, she'd be happy to throw sense, honor, and self respect out into a snow bank to have another night with him.

****

The following day was a series of visitors interrupting the tedium of fittings. Mere Marie had decreed that she wear white, to emphasize her status as a bride to be. It also emphasized the brown of her skin, and when she tried to convey that to the queen, Marie merely snorted.

"Don't hide anything you can't change. Bring it out proudly and stand behind it. Yes, some people will hate you for your skin. Most of France hated me for my birth. I made the mistake, early in my marriage, of backing away from it to try not to offend people. I won't make that mistake again. Carry yourself tall and proud and. I think half an inch lower in the bodice, don't you, Bridget?"

Bridget nodded enthusiastically and started in on the required adjustment.

At the sound of the front door opening and voices, Marie sighed. "Come on down when they finish with the fitting, my dear. We'll show you off to a few dozen more people. Then, I wonder if you will come walking with me before supper."

People in Maine brought small gifts when they came to pay a call, almost always food. It was, of course, good manners to offer them food and tea as well, and to share it with them. By the time the last visitors had left, Grace was thinking that she'd much rather skip supper all together.

The sun was low in the sky when she grabbed a coat, scarf, and gloves and went outside with the exiled queen. Marie was pensive, although she still smiled and took her arm as they walked through the snowy garden. A few bushes still held red berries, although the rest were bare, and the snow had been carefully brushed off a sundial near the house. Someone had spread dried corn for the birds, and a cardinal and a chickadee complained to each other as they scooped it from the frozen snow.

Beyond the garden was a stone wall that made a fair-sized enclosure. It took a few moments for Grace to realize that it was a cemetery, and the snow covered stones marked lives lost or taken.

"My husband was a peculiarly stubborn man. No decisiveness in him, very little passion, and not a bit of cruelty, but he could match anyone in sheer stubbornness. When things were turning bad at the end, he developed our escape plan but could not decide when to use it. He didn't want to leave France, you see. She was his first love, and always his deepest, however much he loved his children. At last, he sent us on ahead to Maine, by ship. I knew it was the last time I'd ever see him. He wasn't a passionate man, but I was always a passionate woman, and I left him with all the passion I could."

She sighed, running her hand over a snow covered gravestone. "I lost one son while we were still in France, another here to small pox before the vaccinations came round. I lost my husband that day we left on the ship, although he wasn't killed for many months after. Loss is hard on anyone, but perhaps worst for a wife and mother." She turned and faced Grace, her face set. "His name isn't Pierre."

Grace blinked and took a step back. "I'm sorry?"

"You need to know before you marry him, if you do. My youngest son was born in Maine, nine months after that last goodbye. His name is Louis Augustus

Pierre, and he is second in line to the empty throne of France, if he cared about such things. I just couldn't risk losing him, too, so I lied. Two of his sisters were adopted. It was easy enough to stay secluded and in mourning through his birth, easy enough to spread the story that the exiled queen in her grief had adopted a third child. No one thought anything of it. I was already eccentric in so many ways that this one more couldn't possibly hurt."

Grace steadied herself against the chill of the stone wall. "Does Pierre— Does he know?"

Marie nodded. "It's his right to know, and he has since he was fourteen. He was grateful to be spared the intrigue and drudgery of royal life. There are so many things that he enjoys better."

Grace snorted and looked at the queen, abashed. "I'm sorry, I meant no disrespect."

Marie trilled out a laugh like sunlight in the form of sound. "Oh, I know what he is like. I love who he is, but I can't say that he's the right temperament to suffer fools gladly. And that's half of what being royalty is."

"But how can you not care then, who he might marry? He's got the blood of two royal families in his veins, and I'm a royal bastard with a dancer for a mother. I don't even know my mother's real name."

"And one of my daughters had a seamstress for a mother before me, and another was a street urchin with no parents at all." Marie reached over to pat her hand. "People believe that the most foolish things are important, which is sad and often infuriating. When one has lost as many people and things as I have, one gains a certain perspective."

Grace shook her head. "You and Charlotte would get along together extremely well."

Marie smiled and turned back to the house. "So my son says. But she is happily married and not in love with my son, so I am happy to have you here instead."

Grace choked, unable to come up with a reply, and instead, followed her back to the house in silence.

****

There was no receiving line at the party, just a gathering room before dinner, where they were welcomed, given drinks, and left to mingle with the other guests. The room was more tasteful than the rooms Grace had seen on her last visit, and she suspected that the Viscount's wife had chosen the décor in there—cream and sage green wall paper, with oak furniture.

Everyone knew everybody else with the notable exception of Grace, who had met a double handful the previous day. She was quite sure that she didn't remember a single name, but no one minded. There were a few dubious glances her way, but no shock or outright hostility.

Everyone knew, long before they got here tonight, what to expect.

Word travelled quickly in a town that size, but she suspected that their hostess had managed to mention the color of her skin to each person she'd invited. It was safer and easier that way.

She recalled a saying from her youth, 'There are no secrets in small towns or large houses.' *I wonder what the servants here know. I wonder what everyone knows, but hasn't thought to question.*

Dinner was done rather differently than she was used to. There were no discrete courses, but servants kept bringing in additional dishes as the meal progressed. There was, as Pierre had warned her, an embarrassment of food. She made sure to taste everything, and taste only, so she wasn't left unable to try later dishes. She was glad when the desserts began to be passed around, as half of them were strange to her, but all delicious.

"You can't get cane sugar most of the year, so we use maple sugar and maple syrup instead," Madame La Grande explained. "I really do prefer it for many things. Try the pecan pie!"

It was foolish to think that someone couldn't be a villain because she was a gracious hostess and kept an excellent chef, but Grace really hoped that the Viscount's wife was ignorant of his actions.

When dinner was over, Pierre came up to her with a glass of champagne and a wide smile. "No one will mind if we disappear together for a few minutes. They'll be disappointed if we don't. We just have to return every ten minutes, for the sake of propriety, and then make conversation for half an hour before we disappear again."

She looked up at him as she took the proffered glass. "That doesn't leave much time for kissing. We'd better search fast." She grinned at the sudden heat in his eyes and sipped the champagne. "Ready when you are," she said, setting the glass down and taking his arm. "I believe you wanted to give me a tour?"

It had been five days and two hours since the last time they had made love, and Grace was fairly sure that she could have recounted the minutes if she bothered to take her watch out of her reticule to check. Being alone with him in the dimly lit hallway made it difficult to concentrate on their mission to find what was going on with the Viscount and what he knew.

Most married men, Grace had learned, kept a room that was theirs alone, a refuge from all things feminine, graceful, or lovely. The library was not it—too welcoming—nor was the writing room with its delicate desk. In the back corner of the house, however, they found a plain room with an ugly wooden desk, brown paneled walls, and a handful of correspondence. Their ten minutes were up, so they merely identified the room and closed the door again. They heard a small sound in the corridor, and then Pierre was taking her into his arms and kissing her quite as passionately as she could wish.

A throat cleared, and there was the sound of moving away, but Grace stole another minute kissing him, gripping his shoulders through his fine jacket, pushing herself close against him until she could feel his warmth. Then she pulled back, smiling.

"Here's to finding what we seek quickly."

"Minx," he mock growled as he took her arm and walked with her back to the drawing room. "You'll certainly be the death of me at this rate."

"But what a way to die," she murmured back before they entered the room and separated to do their duty with conversation.

The half hour was interminable, and they might have cut it short by a few minutes before they snuck out again. Grace saw a great number of knowing looks shot their way, and reflected that Pierre was right; the company would have been disappointed if there had been nothing to happily gossip over.

They went straight to the study, where they split the desk right and left, searching for clues and hidden drawers. Practice with Charlotte's many desks gave Grace an advantage there, and she discovered the false bottom in the middle left drawer within a few minutes. Inside was a bundle of letters bound by twine. They split the pile, and Pierre whistled a few moments later as he read the first.

"They claim to have his sister and her family, alive and in custody. They're offering to send him one of them for every favor he does for Napoleon. After that many years…how can he even know that it's truly her, and that she's still alive?"

"Because they made her write him a letter mentioning a number of childhood memories. Oh, this is heart breaking." Grace looked up. "Family comes first. He might not betray his own queen for this, but he'd certainly betray a queen he feels no connection to."

There was a rattle at the door handle, and Grace wrapped her left arm around Pierre and turned his back to the door as she pulled the pistol from her reticule. The kiss was short and bruising before she stepped out from behind him and pointed the gun at the Viscount.

"Come in and close the door, monsieur. We have a great deal to discuss."

Jules La Grande looked ashen, but he did as she said. "You know," he said, and walked past them to sink into a chair.

"We know that you have a lot to answer for, and we know why you did it," Grace said softly. "We need to know a great deal more."

The Viscount laughed without humor. "You might as well. I've failed everyone."

He pulled an envelope from his pocket and set in down in front of Pierre, who picked it up. "That's my contact information, how I found the Brit who supposedly needed my help. I suspect I may have been set up to take the fall, since they didn't really need my help beyond transportation and a few letters of introduction."

"They?" Grace seized upon.

"The Brit and the woman with him. I never saw her face, but I'd swear he was scared of her, that she was the one running the shots. They used me to deliver a few crates here and there, and he always glanced at her when he told me what they wanted me to do. It was enough that they were supposed to send the whole family—Isabelle, her husband, her son, his wife, and the two grandchildren. But more than likely they lied, and she's never coming."

Pierre pushed him for more details, writing careful notes on the back of the letter from the contact, and then nodded his satisfaction. "Is there anything else you know?"

"The man said something about backup plans, and the woman said not to worry, there was always the day of the speech to finish things. I don't know what speech she meant."

Grace felt her fingers turning numb. "What's today?" she asked urgently.

The Viscount looked at her as though she'd lost her mind, but Pierre answered immediately. "It's Saturday, November the twenty-sixth."

Grace drew in a ragged breath. "The queen's speech is Monday. We have only thirty six hours to stop whatever they have planned, and even changing horses, there's no way to do it."

"We'll take a boat," Pierre said briskly. "We'll head to the port immediately."

"Nothing will leave before morning, right?"

"Yes, that's right."

"Then we've something else we need to do." She turned her attention to the Viscount. "You need to write a full confession of everything you've done, and sign it, throwing yourself on the queen's mercy. If we get there in time, you've a good chance of receiving it. Then, since we've been here far longer than ten minutes, you're going to walk us out to the company and announce that, as my own father is an ocean away, you felt the need to speak with both of us about our engagement to satisfy yourself that Pierre will make an excellent husband despite his somewhat wild nature."

"Me?" Pierre objected.

Grace ignored him. "You will publicly give us your blessing, and we will share a kiss in front of the assembled crowd. Soon after, we'll take the queen home and head to the port from there. Everything will be happy, no one's night will be ruined, and nobody outside this room needs to know anything until the queen makes her judgment."

Viscount La Grande sighed, and reached for an inkbottle. "That's better than I deserve, honestly." He looked up at Pierre. "This one's a gem, my boy. Tough as nails and soft as butter. Don't let her go."

"I won't," Pierre promised.

It was a brief confession, but it contained all the pertinent information, and a few minutes later, the Viscount was making his grand announcement, smiling and waving his hand as if he hadn't a care in the world.

We all play roles in life, don't we? When have I ever just been myself? With Charlotte, except I'm still her Lady in Waiting. And with Pierre.

Twenty minutes later, covered with well wishes, they and the queen were on their way back out into the cold. It was warmer than the last dreadful night of their journey there, but still stubbornly below freezing, and Marie exclaimed in distress as they filled her in on recent developments.

"I'm not sure a ship will be able to leave in this cold," she fretted.

"It's our only chance to warn her," Grace told her. "We'll be as safe as we can be, but we need to try."

Marie nodded slowly. "I know you do. I won't ask either of you to be less than you are...but come home to me."

Pierre hugged her from his side, and Grace impulsively embraced her from hers as well. When they reached the house, Pierre jumped down and lifted the others down before the coachman could do more than stop the horses.

They raced into the house, and Grace called out, "Don't forget a scarf!"

Pierre laughed as he took the stairs two at a time. "I'll bring two," he promised. "Dress as warmly as you can."

Bridget acted as if it were the most natural thing in the world for people to come home from a party and immediately set out into the night. She found two pairs of silk undergarments that covered Grace from ankles and wrists to her neck and buttoned together at the waist, put both her petticoats on over that, and then the warmer traveling dress before adding wool stockings, boots, gloves, her good wool coat, a scarf, her hat, and another scarf to tie the hat down. It felt rather ridiculous, but remembering that bitterly cold ride to get there, Grace could hardly protest.

She transferred her gun into one pocket of the great coat, and her watch into the other, then slipped her reticule into the nearly empty valise and turned to head back downstairs. "Thank you, Bridget. I hope to see you again soon."

"Oh, I'm sure you will, miss, after the wedding."

Grace tried not to grimace. *Yes, and I certainly fueled those fires tonight.* Still, she couldn't think of another way she could have handled things nearly as smoothly.

Marie was already waiting by the door with a packet of food, and the sleigh was waiting outside with fresh horses and a different coachman.

"I don't want you to go hungry," she explained. "It's a mother's constant fear."

Grace hugged her again, and then Pierre was coming down the stairs, as well wrapped as she was.

"We should be able to get a boat from the harbor if the seas cooperate. That's about an hour away."

She nodded her understanding and headed outside as he gave his mother one more hug. The coachman helped her in, Pierre jumped in beside her, and they were off.

It was closing in on midnight, and the coachman was driving cautiously rather than quickly on the icy road. The small swerves of the sleigh as he corrected the horses reminded her how precarious the roads were, and how slow the travel. They had two hundred and ten miles to travel, which would take nine days by post and nine hours by train. With neither post nor train available. It had taken them four days with good horses and more than their share of good luck, and they had only thirty-five hours now to do it.

"We'll make it," Pierre told her, grabbing onto her hand and squeezing. "There will be a boat, and if there isn't, we'll think of something else."

It was a crazy promise to make, but she took comfort from it anyway. *We won't give up,* she translated. *No matter what, we'll keep trying, together.*

She knew before they even reached the port that there were going to be complications. The wind was rising, and the waves were taller than she'd expected, with clumps of ice bobbing, white in the dark harbor.

The waterfront was full of noises, none of them human. Ships creaked as the waves hit them, water splashed, and sails flapped in the wind. A few gaslights sent more shadows than light, but the masts of the ships were visible with the sails looking like ghosts, while the ice in the water below looked like poorly sketched reflections.

Pierre swore softly in French as he surveyed the scene and directed the coachman to pull up in front of the largest ship there, a merchantman flying English colors. He jumped out before they had quite stopped and started speaking rapidly to the man on duty by the gangplank. The man argued a moment, then turned and disappeared into the ship. Pierre returned to help Grace down, and they waited together at the bottom of the gangplank.

"He's waking the captain, which no one likes to do, but I impressed upon him that this is serious. I don't like the look of the water, but we'll see what the captain says. We can try driving to the next Port to the south, but that's a good four hours."

She reached out to squeeze his arm. "We'll find a way," she echoed him. *We won't give up, no matter what.*

The captain, when he came, was an Englishman a few years younger than Pierre.

"I wish I could help you," he replied, "but only a fool would set out in this sea, and it'll likely be two days before we can sail again."

"It's for Her Majesty, Queen Charlotte," Grace pressed.

The captain shook his head. "I'd happily help a much lesser person, but I can't change the sea even for Her Majesty. We were supposed to land in Boston and had to divert because of weather. There's actually a shipment for Her Majesty on board, some foolish gift from Parliament—mechanical horses."

Grace caught her breath. "Could we see them?" she asked carefully.

Pierre and the captain both looked at her, the former with interest, and the latter as if she had gone mad.

The captain nodded. "I suppose so." He called an order and led them on deck and to an enclosed platform behind the mast.

Grace peeked in when he opened the door and let her breath out in a sigh. Two black stallions stood at attention, the steamworks within glowing red from their eyes and where their joints met.

"We need them," she told Pierre. "This is the other way we said we'd find."

"Steam powered horses? They'll never handle the snow and the roads."

"These will. They're designed for hunting. They can go overland, jump, even ford a river if it isn't too deep. And they can travel twenty miles per hour without tiring."

She let that echo for a moment—as fast as a train, through places no train could go.

The captain cleared his throat. "I'm sorry, but it's not in my power to give them to you, or even to sell them to you. They're sent expressly to Her Majesty by both houses of Parliament, and I don't have the authority to release them anywhere else."

Grace smiled. "Ah, but I do." She produced the ring, and fished in her valise for the paper from Charlotte. "There can be no blame to you for following the queen's direct order."

"What are they going to pull, at those speeds?" Pierre asked as the captain studied the paper and handed it back. "That would send a sleigh over at the first good rock."

"We'll ride them. They have saddles as well as rigging. I wouldn't call it safe, but certainly much safer than a carriage or sleigh would be."

Pierre shook his head, but not in disagreement, and the captain sighed.

"I wish you the best with your mission, and hope I never have to explain this to my superiors. We'll get them offloaded within the hour."

"Thank you, sir. You truly are doing the right thing," Grace reassured him.

She followed Pierre down the gangplank to collect their belongings before sending the coachman home with the accurate, if incomplete, information that they had indeed found transportation to Boston.

"I'm not surprised that the House of Lords did this, but I'm disappointed that the House of Commons went along with it."

Pierre raised an eyebrow. "It seems a princely gift."

"Oh, it is. They're identical to the pair that encouraged her father, the Prince Regent, to get himself killed with his racing curricle. Flesh and blood horses have limits, and some sense of self-preservation. These don't. They aren't just a gift to the queen—they're a warning. 'Know your limits. You too can fall.'"

Chapter Sixteen

The horses were eerily silent until given the command to come to attention, then stamped and blew and flicked their tails in an uncanny imitation of life, if only they had not done so in perfect unison.

Neither of the saddles was designed for skirts, and Grace reluctantly slit both the petticoats to keep her legs covered as she rode, while the traveling dress itself hiked up to her knees. The undergarments and wool stockings were more crucial than ever, but there was a faint warmth from the horses that helped to dispel the cold. They fastened the small bags behind them and set out into the night.

It had taken an hour from the main road to the port by the sleigh, but it took ten minutes on the horses. Their mechanical hooves seemed to effortlessly find purchase on the snow and ice, and their stride never varied.

It was hard to talk to each other at such a speed. The wind of their passage stole Grace's breath, and she just bent her head and held on, trusting Pierre to guide them through the darkness of the night.

In other circumstances, it would have been exhilarating—the boundless power, the glow of the red eyes, the ice white of the stars above and the ground below. All she could think about was the distance and the price if they failed.

They stopped at dawn for warm drinks and hot food in Brunswick, and she marveled that they had travelled two day's rapid journey in a few hours. She could barely feel her legs when they first stopped, but stomping around soon restored them.

"We need to save our strength," she told Pierre. "I should lead for the next few hours, so you can conserve yourself for later." She paused and looked up at him over her plate of hash and potato leek pie. "You do have a gun on you, don't you? It hasn't come up."

He laughed, taking her hand. "Please, please marry me, Grace, because there is not another woman in the world like you."

She flushed and pulled her hand back, smiling. "A simple yes or no would suffice."

"Yes. You've just always gotten to yours first."

She shook her head. "You'll have to work on that."

They mounted the horses, which were causing people to stop and stare even in the large city, and she took the lead as she'd said. It was easier in daylight, but even through the layers, the wind at the speed of their passing cut through her clothing like a knife. She focused on keeping them in the middle of the road when there was no one else in sight and slowed them from their highest speed only when they encountered other traffic. The places they'd passed on their four day journey seemed to fly by, and by noon, they were in Portland again. They paused at an inn for a quick meal and stretch, and then Grace was grateful to have Pierre take over the lead.

"How are you doing?" he asked as they pulled back out onto the road.

"I'm fine," she shouted back.

It was all relative. He was as sore and exhausted as she was, but they could both keep going. Nothing else mattered.

The miles continued. They went through Portsmouth without stopping, and paused in Amesbury only for a few minutes for a warm drink and to shake the road out of their muscles. The innkeeper there remembered them, and offered them a room for the night, but with the mechanical horses, they were close enough to keep going.

It was full dark as they approached Boston, and they could see the city from miles off, an irregular patchwork of light with the present gaslights mapping out where the streets were. They slowed the horses and rode single file through the crowded streets, gaslights gleaming on the black metal. A few people called out and pointed, but Boston was too jaded for anything less than an exploding airship to captivate people for long.

Finally, they pulled up in front of the governor's mansion, and Grace belatedly remembered that the governor himself was one of their suspects.

"We have to be as nonchalant about our arrival as possible," she murmured.

"We just rode over two hundred miles in a single day on horses that look like something straight out of a nightmare," he murmured back. "I'm happy to follow your lead."

Grace snorted, and jumped down from her horse to knock on the door with the enormous brass ring. The door opened to reveal the butler, who certainly had had more irregular moments during their visit than in his whole career before.

"Could you tell Her Majesty that we're delivering a present to her from Parliament?" she asked the butler. He looked at her with reproach—he recognized her and knew she was to be admitted, but also knew that her manners ought to be better.

"The household is seated at supper," he informed her.

"Oh, bother!" Grace replied, trying not to sound relieved. "Well, let's have these put in the stables for safekeeping, and we'll show her tomorrow. Could you have a room made up for Mr. Beauchamp, please? Then we'll both take trays in our rooms, so as not to disrupt the household."

Her request was more in keeping with the dignity of the house, and the butler nodded his assent before directing an underling to take the mechanical horses.

Pierre raised an eyebrow at her. "I do have a room in Boston, you know," he whispered.

"And how will that help us devise our plan of attack for tomorrow?" Grace murmured back. "I'll talk to you later."

She was so sore from the riding that climbing the stairs was its own form of agony, but she had too much pride to show it. A quick glance at Pierre showed that he, too, was climbing with unusual precision, and she took unreasonable comfort from that. *I don't want to slow him down. I don't want to tie him down. I want to be his partner, not his dependent.*

Her room looked so familiar and safe—despite the memory of the spiders—that she almost cried. When Milly showed up, she did cry a little with the relief of being taken care of. Milly asked no difficult questions but brought her tea and a meal, drew her a hot bath, and brushed out her hair as she soaked in the warm water. By the time she was wrapped up in a dressing gown, there was a knock on the door, and Charlotte came in. She was still dressed for dinner, her hair up and a strand of rubies around her neck. Her eyes were tired, but her smile was warm and bright.

"Oh, my dear," Charlotte said, opening her arms. "Tell me all about it."

Milly discreetly let herself out, and Grace obliged. Charlotte predictably brushed off the news of the plans for her assassination and insisted on the hearing the whole story from the very beginning. She included the affair, even the realization that she had forgotten proper precautions on the one occasion. The only thing she left out was Mere Marie's revelation about Pierre's parentage, and she realized that, for the first time, she had a loyalty that might conflict with her loyalty to Charlotte.

When she had finished, Charlotte sat in silence for a moment, then scrawled a note on a piece of paper, folded and sealed it, and rang the bell for a servant. Milly appeared a few moments later, and Charlotte handed the note to her.

"Give this to Mr. Beauchamp, please," she instructed, and Milly curtsied and hurried away.

"What did you write?" Grace asked, curious.

"I told him to come to your bedchamber without being seen to talk to both of us."

Grace snorted. "That's very direct."

Charlotte frowned. "The speech is in twelve hours. We don't have time to be anything less."

There was no arguing with that, so Grace just nodded and tried not to obsess over the fact that she was in her dressing gown, barefoot, her hair loose down her back, and about to have a conversation with both her lover and her queen.

"What happened while I was gone?" she asked.

Charlotte grimaced. "A fair bit from Verity and David, but nothing from anyone else. They travelled on the airship to London and returned yesterday. Verity was able to identify the maker, and one of their masters is conveniently away with an ill relative. His description doesn't match the second man that Emma saw, however. So it's likely that there are still more people involved. Him, the Viscount, the Brit, as Le Grande described the other man, and this unknown woman, at least."

Grace hesitated. "Do you think it might be Miss Farnsworth?"

Charlotte hesitated. "My instinct says no, but I don't dare trust it fully with this much at stake."

There was a tiny sound at the window, and Grace had the gun in her hand before she realized she'd moved. Charlotte looked at her with a raised eyebrow.

"When this is over, you need a vacation," she said, and crossed to the window to open it.

Pierre slid in, wearing the same black outfit he'd worn the last time he'd come in that way, and Grace wondered where he'd managed to pack it that she hadn't noticed.

"Ah, a third time you point a gun at me," Pierre exclaimed melodramatically, one hand on his heart. "This is clearly proof that we were meant to be."

Grace's lips twitched, and Charlotte laughed.

"Please, sit down, Mr. Beauchamp," Charlotte ordered. "We have a great deal to talk about, and not a great deal of time. I'm speaking at Faneuil Hall tomorrow, and I understand that someone intends to make sure that I don't survive the experience."

"Several someones, I'd say. I don't believe you have anything to fear from Viscount La Grande, but the other two are unaccounted for."

"Three," Charlotte murmured.

Pierre sat up straighter. "Three?" he asked neutrally.

"A master steamworker from the house that altered the spiders is absent for family reasons, which we presume to mean that he is actually here somewhere. The spiders were altered only a few days before they attacked."

Grace nodded at his questioning look, and he sighed.

"You have to cancel the speech, Your Majesty," he told her. "That's too many variables for us to be able to keep you safe."

Charlotte shook her head firmly. "That's not an option. This is hugely important. Legislatures from all fifteen colonies will be present, and it is the best and only opportunity I have to move things forward."

"With all respect, Your Majesty, you can't fix the ills of the world if you are dead," Pierre bit out.

Charlotte smiled. "I can't change the world at all if I'm afraid. If I fall, someone else will stand up. If I run, nothing will ever get better."

Pierre groaned. "You are so much like my mother that it makes my head hurt."

"Thank you. I would love to meet her," Charlotte said serenely. "Now, how are we going to do our best to have our pudding and eat it, too? Given the choice, I'd really prefer not to die tomorrow."

Grace frowned. "The two of us will be there of course, armed and ready, but that's not nearly enough. May I call on Verity and David?"

"They'll both be there anyway, but if there is any way they might be able to help, certainly." Charlotte nodded. "And I will compromise and wear that hideous corset that stops shrapnel and beams, so I'll survive a chest shot if it comes to that."

Pierre sighed. "I'll go over the building in the morning before the speech to look for bombs or likely hiding places for crazed assassins. But it's not the crazed assassins that worry me, it's the professionals. And the people behind this can afford the best."

Once again, Grace remembered how much Miss Farnsworth's long, slender fingers, reminded her of the deceased Evelyn. She was young to already be a professional assassin, but Evelyn had been younger still when she began working for Charlotte.

"We'll make it happen," Grace said bracingly. "We made it here in thirteen hours from Belfast, Maine. I'm not calling anything impossible from this day forward."

Charlotte leaned forward and kissed her on the forehead, then rose. "I will leave my life in your capable hands." She smiled but said nothing else as she exited the room.

"Do you feel as intimidated as I do right now?" Pierre asked.

Grace grinned. "Almost certainly." She took a step forward and paused.

"I don't want to risk more than we already have," she said. "Not until we know."

"I respect that. So do we play it smart or torture each other for a bit first?"

Grace untied the belt to her dressing gown and let it fall to the floor. "Torture sounds good to me."

He stepped closer. "There are limits to my self control, so I'm keeping my clothes on."

She stood in front of him in the translucent shift and smiled, running one hand over the most sensitive part of his anatomy through the thin silk. "I think I can work with that." She pulled one strap over her shoulder, then the other, and let the shift pool at her feet before stepping free.

He groaned and pulled her close, his mouth fastening on hers while his hands ran down her back to her buttocks. She rubbed herself against him, feeling his heat and stroking him again with her hand.

He picked her up and lifted her onto the bed, stretching out beside her to stroke her body as his mouth traveled down her neck and fastened on one breast. He gave a quick suck, and she moaned.

"Let me know if I hurt you," he whispered.

She shook her head. "I don't think you could."

She pulled up his head to kiss him and rubbed her naked body against the silk of his clothing until it was only by the layer of fabric that they were not mating. "I wanted to do this that night," she confessed. "I wanted you, even though of course I didn't trust you."

He paused, looking into her eyes. "And now?"

"I trust you with my life." She looked back, nothing hidden. "I trust you with Charlotte's life."

He buried his face in her hair and started, slowly and gently, to caress her skin. Her arms, her breasts, her belly, and then gently between her legs until she sighed and parted them. His mouth fastened again on the breast, but softer this time, in rhythm with the gentle stroking until she felt herself slowly catching fire, burning, burning. The flames ran higher until they washed over her in waves of release, and she opened her eyes, surprised to find her body still intact.

She smiled tentatively at him. "Thank you. But I didn't do anything for you."

He shook his head and kissed her. "No, love. You gave me everything." He pulled the covers up over her. "Now sleep. We'll talk tomorrow, after we save the world and England."

Chapter Seventeen

It was indecently early when Grace knocked at Verity's front door, but she was not at all surprised to find the other woman already up and working in her workshop.

"With the ceremony to go to today, not to mention dressing for it and all the fuss after, I knew I wouldn't get anything useful done if I didn't start early," she explained.

"I'm afraid I have another distraction for you," Grace apologized, and explained what little they knew about the assassination plot.

"So . . . it could be bombs, more spiders, guns . . . pretty much anything?" Verity asked. She grimaced at Grace's nod. "Well, there's nothing like a challenge to wake you up in the morning. I already have Rufus and his friends trained to recognize the spiders, and I should be able to program in the basic explosives this morning, but I can't have them attacking everyone with guns when you, David, and likely others on our side will be using them. I can instruct them to sit on people who look dangerous, but I'll have to do that with one verbal command at a time."

"It's a wonderful help," Grace assured her. "Her Majesty has complete confidence in us."

"That somehow fails to make me feel even the slightest bit better," Verity confessed. "Maybe it will inspire David, though. He's much more of a white knight than I am. Which, I guess, makes today appropriate." She grimaced again. "Charlotte . . . Her

Majesty warned us that it's going to happen, probably to make sure we're there and dressed appropriately."

Grace laughed. "Yes, that was almost certainly her thought in giving you warning. And she trusted that you wouldn't turn tail and run at the news."

Verity harrumphed. "If it were me, instead of David, I might very well have. He's far better at this than I am. I'm much happier in an apron and with ink splotches on my fingers. Really, all I want is an ordinary life with the man I love, and a few children in time. Well that, and a well-stocked workroom to create in."

An ordinary life with the man I love. "Not all of us get what we want," Grace said gently. "But we get the chance to make the best of what we have."

Verity looked at her sharply. "There is more going on than a mere assassination attempt, isn't there? Not with the queen. With you."

Grace smiled crookedly. "There is, but if I tell you about it now, you won't have time to program the dogs, we'll miss the ceremony, and the best monarch England's had in centuries will likely be dead. How about tea tomorrow?"

"Here," Verity said firmly. "I'll have the cook make chocolate scones, and if necessary, we'll have sherry with our tea."

Grace smiled more firmly. "Thank you. Tea with a friend is exactly what I need, and sherry and chocolate scones are a nice addition. I'll look forward to it. We just have to get through today."

Verity nodded. "At least any assassins will distract me from the whole public appearance piece," she said cheerfully. "If I manage to get shot . . . just a small flesh wound, you understand . . . I might get to miss it altogether."

Grace was still smiling as the carriage took her back to the governor's mansion. She tried to calm her breathing as she prepared for the ceremony; nerves wouldn't make anything easier.

Faneuil Hall was immense, a seven-story structure, complete with galleries and a cupola that alone could have hidden a dozen assassins. A full thousand people were expected, from politicians to journalists to prominent citizens far and near. It was the perfect place for a major announcement to reach the maximum number of people at once. It was also perfect for an assassination. Nearly all of those thousand people would have a reasonably clear shot at the queen, who would be easily visible on the raised stage.

Charlotte, to Grace's surprise, had asked her to wear white, just as the deposed French queen had two days before. Since Charlotte was unlikely to be considering the bride angle, it meant that it suited her purpose for Grace's brown skin to be on obvious display. Trusting Charlotte was second nature to Grace, but knowing that she might very well be in a shooting match while wearing the color was a trifle dispiriting.

I'll be an easy target, and both blood and dirt will be visible from across the entire hall. I'm not sure which part disturbs me more.

She saw Pierre as she entered, and again during the several times in the quarter hour it took her to finally reach her seat on the dais behind where Charlotte would be. She did have an excellent view there of nearly everyone who'd be able to shoot Charlotte, and Pierre took up a position along one of the side walls where he'd have a good view of anyone she couldn't see.

Verity and David arrived soon after, but their placement on the other side of the dais meant that she was unable to talk with them. Verity waved and smiled, then gestured subtly at the half dozen mechanical dogs that looked like statues around the building.

They had reinforcements.

It would have to do.

Grace made out a handful of darker skinned people among the sea of whites, and even a few who looked like red Indians in European style clothing. She saw the Paul family, and said a silent prayer that no harm would come to them.

More people came in. She saw the governor ascend the dais and was happy that his wandering eyes were some distance from her. Mr. Franklin, Mr. Adams, and a few others whose names she couldn't recall were there, too, while the seats and galleries were a sea of strangers.

At last, the movement had slowed to a trickle, the band struck up, and a hush fell over the crowd as "God Save the Queen" played. The crowd stood and joined in, singing with more enthusiasm than accuracy. As they came to the end, Charlotte half-stepped out onto the dais.

"My people," she said simply. "It has been my honor and my joy to live among you for these recent weeks. It was important to me that I come to understand you more intimately than the ocean between us usually allows. I have come to see your strength, your pride, your courage, and your ingenuity. I see why Boston is called the Athens of the Americas, and why you value so the virtues of honor, integrity, and self-reliance.

"I have seen all of this, and I see that America needs laws and governance that reflects her nature. I do not intend to treat you as a lesser cousin, as some before have proposed, nor do I intend to abandon you. Instead, I wish to collaborate with you on your progress, on making this city, and this country, truly a shining city on a hill that all the world may admire.

"In that interest, it is time for one small change. To date, all governors of the fifteen colonies have been Englishmen, appointed by England. Instead, it is time for the governors to be American, chosen by the people they serve. Your other politicians will continue to send delegations to England and participate in the larger government there."

There was a soft rumble of voices, and then, a shot rang out, landing a foot from the queen. Grace followed it back, tracking and looking, and shouts of alarm began to rise up.

"Other changes for this land have taken even more thought," Charlotte went on serenely. "England will end slavery in totality at the New Year, but such an action in America would be horribly disruptive to everyone involved, from slaves to masters to the free workers, white and negro. Instead, We have devised a method that We hope will allow a transition that will benefit all."

Another shot, and the people watched in horror, but were seemingly held silent by the queen's calm.

Grace identified the shooter, and shot even as she watched the man fall from Pierre's blast. A quick survey of the room showed no immediate dangers, so she put the pistol on her lap and returned her gaze pointedly to the queen.

"It is our policy, in England, that no man or woman should bear indentured servitude for more than seven years. From this day forth that shall be the law for whites, negroes, Chinese, and red Indians. No child under the age of fourteen can be indentured, and at the end of seven years, the former servant must be given land and the tools to work it, or the tools to set up in their craft, as already set by law.

"To avoid a sudden surge of workers before the surroundings are ready to absorb them, there will be a reduction in taxes each year for those who free slaves now and release them from service with the appropriate money and tools to start their new lives, on up to one quarter of an owner's slaves per year."

Another shot rang out, the beam singeing the arm of Charlotte's dress, and still, she never flinched. Grace saw David sight the shooter in the right most gallery and followed his shot. It only winged the man, who shot wildly again. She focused her gaze, whispered a single word of prayer, and squeezed the trigger. The shooter fell from the gallery among the crowd below, and a few more screams broke out. Charlotte was still talking, and Grace lowered the gun to her lap again.

"All of these changes, in writing, will be sent to every colony. You will have opportunities to express any concerns that you may have. For today, I would like to thank Governor Spencer for his service, but I will be appointing a temporary governor to this colony until elections can be drawn up and held. Will Mr. Benjamin Franklin Junior please join me on the stage?"

To his credit, Mr. Franklin crossed the dais as calmly as if there hadn't been two shooters so far, and the possibility of more to come. He accepted the queen's appointment with a bow, and then turned to the audience.

"If anyone here does not feel that our queen also exemplifies what is best in America, you haven't been paying attention. We value our courage, our strength, and our determination. May I say, we indeed have a queen worthy of the best we can offer."

There was a roar from the crowd, and they stood and applauded.

When a third shooter rose from the crowd, Grace and the others never had a chance to shoot. The people around him tore him down where he stood.

Charlotte stood serenely for a few minutes, waiting for the cheering to quiet. "Today," she went on, quite as if nothing had happened, "I am privileged to share with you one of the happiest times of being a monarch. The opportunity to reward those whose courage, skill, or determination have made our world brighter. Today, I would like to introduce you to two people who have acted with integrity and fearlessness. I personally owe them a great debt. In England, I would settle on them a peerage for what they have done, but in America, it is fitting that each generation earn their own titles. Please meet Sir David James and Dame Verity James, who is the first

American woman to be knighted, but certainly not the last."

If looks could kill, Verity would have been far more accurate than any of the would-be assassins. Still, she rose and smiled with her husband, knelt to receive the honor, and bowed her thanks to the watching crowd.

"For those of you who might have noticed a slight disruption in tonight's ceremony…" Charlotte paused to allow the laughter to ripple through the crowd. "It should come as no surprise that there are others among us who we must thank today. For tireless courage, unwavering dedication, and excellent aim, let me now introduce to you Sir Pierre Beauchamp and Dame Grace FitzGeorge."

For one eternal moment, Grace thought that she had heard wrong, but Verity was gesturing to her pointedly, so she rose to her feet and came to stand beside Pierre in front of Charlotte.

"Can you accept me as your queen, not in place of, but in addition to the one you already have?" Charlotte asked too softly for the crowd to hear.

Pierre nodded, and both he and Grace knelt.

The ceremonial sword came down on both his shoulders, on both of Grace's, and then Charlotte gestured for them to rise.

"Arise, Sir Pierre and Lady Grace." She kissed them each on both cheeks, her eyes just a little sad.

The queen never grants a knighthood for anyone's pleasure. It is always and only for the good of the realm.

Charlotte bid her people farewell and the band played again. Grace followed Charlotte out, down the central aisle through the throng, smiling, waving, and pressing hands. Verity whistled as she followed, and the crowd gasped as the six bronze dogs suddenly stood and followed her.

Grace nabbed both Verity and Pierre and pulled them into her carriage, trusting David to follow his wife. "Will your dogs follow the carriage?" she asked Verity. "I don't think we have room for them."

"Yes, they'll follow me," Verity reassured her. "Am I the only one who attends a formal ceremony without a gun?"

"You don't generally need one," her husband reminded her.

Verity sighed. "I'm a trifle disappointed that the dogs didn't get to do anything."

Grace snorted. "And I'm grateful. That was more than enough for one day. Did any of you get a good look at the shooters? Was one of them the steamworker you were trying to find?"

"No, but someone of his description was fished out of the river this morning," David replied a trifle grimly. "I think his usefulness had come to an end. It looked as if he was poisoned."

"There's a certain grim poetic justice to that," Verity sighed.

"One of the three assassins at the ceremony fit the description of the second man," Pierre added in. "He'd be the British man, so likely, the contact that brought in the steamworker. The other two looked like hired thugs."

Grace sighed. "So all we're missing is the woman." She shook her head, thinking. "I didn't see Miss Farnsworth at the ceremony, did you?"

Pierre looked at her sharply. "Do you really suspect Miss Farnsworth?"

"Do you have a good reason that I shouldn't?"

He hesitated, then shook his head. "I'm quite sure she'd never betray my mother, although, that is a story that isn't mine to tell. I don't know that she wouldn't betray your— Charlotte, if she had reason enough."

It warmed her inexplicably that he no longer referred to Charlotte as 'your queen', but she fought to stay focused. "So today was a great success, except that there is at least one conspirator still on the loose. Who is not necessarily Miss Farnsworth and could, in fact, be anyone."

Verity sighed. "How long will the reception at the governor's mansion last? I'm already tired."

"You're one of the guests of honor. That means staying anything under two hours is actually rude. Two and a half is safer," her husband informed her.

"So why don't we all run away to our place after two hours and thirty one minutes?" Verity asked. "I won't have the chocolate scones today, but there's always sherry."

Grace laughed. "We can have sherry at the reception if you like. It's the peace and quiet at your house that's so appealing."

They pulled up at the mansion, and Pierre jumped out to help Grace and Verity down. Verity whistled to the following dogs, and they abandoned the carriage to follow her into the foyer, where she arranged them out of the way and set them back in standby mode.

"The reception is in the ballroom," Grace informed the others. "If we weren't all obligated to be there, I would recommend watching from the balconies. You just go up the stair case here and they're on either side."

Verity sighed. "We'll do our duty with a smile on our faces or die trying. Lay on, Macduff!"

"You do know that the Scottish play is not considered appropriate reading for ladies, don't you?" David teased her.

Verity snorted. "If Grace and I stuck to the things considered appropriate for ladies, Her Majesty might be dead now."

"I think we need to rework the concept of 'lady' to fit the modern era," Grace commented. She wrinkled her nose. "How about 'a lady follows her own innate good taste without regard to society or convention?'"

The ballroom seemed larger set up for the reception than it had during the ball. *Was it only the week before?* Tables of food and drink were scattered throughout the room, encouraging people to pause and mingle rather than dance.

Verity looked up at the galleries, frowning. "I don't think I even noticed them during the ball. Do you think anyone will notice if I go look at them?"

Grace shook her head. "Not if you hurry. People are only just starting to arrive."

Verity grinned and vanished, and Grace looked around the room, trying not to sigh. Two hours and thirty-one minutes seemed more than fair, except that she owed Charlotte more than that. *How much more, and for how long? And how can I even think that way, after all she's done for me?*

She picked up a glass of champagne, mostly because she knew the bubbles would keep her from drinking it too quickly. Pierre was watching her, and she forced a smile.

"What's wrong?" he asked her softly.

I killed a man today. I was made a knight. Not because I deserve it, although I probably do, but because the color of my skin and my gender make it a good thing for the realm. I want an ordinary life with the man I love, and I don't think that's possible, even if you love me back.

"I'm just a little tired," she said. "It's been a long day. A long week. A long month, since the first day I met you, since I came to America."

"Do you want to go home?" he asked.

Tears pricked at her eyes, and she blinked them away, her smile fiercer. "Bastards, as a rule, don't have homes," she answered, harsher than he deserved. "Excuse me." She walked away before she could cry, before she could say something she'd truly regret.

She made determined polite conversation to person after person, occasionally running into Verity who would recite the number of minutes left until they could decently leave as if it were a prayer or a magic spell. She noticed Miss Farnsworth was present, but her suspicions seemed foolish, empty now. There was a certain let down that the ordeal was over.

The Pauls were there, although they had to leave early. They were more sober than she expected, and Mrs. Paul explained why.

"It's a good step, and a necessary step, but it's going to make things quite a bit worse for quite a lot of people before they start getting better. Right now, slaves may be mistreated, but they're also valuable property, and people think of them that way. You wouldn't harm your neighbor's horses or cattle, after all. Free blacks are perhaps a tenth of the population of the slaves, and so we are an oddity, too rare to be threatening. Take away that protection and that rarity . . . and people are going to be threatened. It may go more smoothly, doing it gradually. Certainly, the Northern organizations can help more when it's fewer people at a time, but this isn't the end. It's just the first step in the beginning."

Grace sighed. "So that's why Her Majesty . . ." Her voice trailed off as she realized she was being indiscreet, but Mrs. Paul nodded.

"Her Majesty acknowledged you, a negro, as a person of value, independent of wealth or birth or even gender. Of course, that was calculated, as was the timing. She's doing her honest best to change the world without destroying it. She's just going to need all the help we can give."

Grace hugged them goodbye. *I'm part of something huge. It's terrifying and overwhelming, but it matters.*

She was reaching for a second glass of champagne when someone screamed.

Miss Farnsworth was standing on a chair, a gun in her hand, pointed straight at the queen. A hush fell, and Charlotte held out her hands to the girl.

"You don't want to do this, Sophia."

"Oh, I most definitely do," Miss Farnsworth said grimly. "Please be so kind as to duck, your Majesty."

Charlotte threw herself flat without hesitation, and Miss Farnsworth shot repeatedly at the metallic spider directly behind her on the wall.

Verity whistled sharply and went to the main doors to let in her dogs, only to find the doors locked. Grace shifted the gun that was already in her hand, looking for a target. A voice from the gallery above startled her.

"Well, now, that was foolish of you, Sophia. That one would have taken care of the queen, and probably only a few of the rest of you would have died. Now, I'll have to take care of all of you."

The voice, horribly, was Mrs. Woodward, but not at all sane.

"I tried to be patient. First, my idiot father gave up his title, and then my idiot husband, and for what? Some foolish dream of equality, which means we're no better than servants, negroes, and red Indians. Equality is for fools. I had plans to better myself, better my children…and there are plenty of people in England willing to give a title in return for service. But not the queen, no. She's as deluded as the rest of you, and that's why she has to die. And, you too, of course. Don't worry. It doesn't take long at all for the poison to kill you."

Grace tried squeezing off a shot at the shadows where the voice came from, but Mrs. Woodward only laughed.

"Naughty, naughty." There were spiders climbing down on all sides and the people started to crowd into the middle. "So sorry to leave the party early, but I know you won't miss me."

Verity put her hands on her hips and called out firmly. "Sheba, Rufus. Sit!"

There was a thud and a scream from above, but Grace didn't have time to figure out what had happened. Spiders were nearing the floor, and she found herself beside Miss Farnsworth, shooting spider after spider.

"Beam weapons only stun them!" she called out to the people near her.

Pierre ran by with a dagger in one hand and a serving tray held like a shield in the other. "We've shared this dance before, love."

"By all means, monsieur, let us dance." She kept shooting, counting the seconds before the creatures began to move again, and shooting them once more.

One of Verity's dogs made it up to the gallery and jumped down onto one of the tables, which collapsed beneath its weight. The bronze Rottweiler shook itself and began chasing down spiders, flipping them up and crushing them in its massive jaws.

There were seven destroyed, ten, fourteen… "How many did she have?" Grace wailed.

"I've counted thirty-nine so far, so it depends if they were sold in tens or in dozens or half-dozens. Best case is forty, worst is probably forty-eight," David said cheerfully, still shooting.

Pierre and the bronze dog were the only ones who seemed able to destroy them, and the three of them, with their beam weapons were slowing them down. Mr. Franklin was using his cane like a cricket bat to swing away those that approached, and

Charlotte had the poker from the fireplace. The rest of the generous crowd mostly tried to stay out of the way.

One moved close to Pierre, and Grace swore as she threw herself forward to shoot it. That left a momentary gap, and as she turned, she saw in horror that one had managed to land on Charlotte's chest.

"No!" she screamed.

Pierre turned, while she was still struggling to stand, sending the tray at Charlotte and knocking the thing to the ground.

"Did it get you?" he asked urgently.

Charlotte made a most indelicate denial. "I'm wearing the thrice damned corset, remember! Stop worrying about me and kill these things!"

Miss Farnsworth shot one as it leapt for Grace, and Grace scrambled back to her feet, shaken.

I didn't remember the corset, either. But I thought about Pierre before I thought about Charlotte.

There was no time for thought, just more shooting. Twenty were dead, thirty, thirty-nine. They could find no more, but Grace was not reassured. No one sold such things by the baker's dozen.

They broke through the door, with the help of Charlotte's poker, and Verity sent the three dogs still there hunting for spiders throughout the house, then turned to run up the stairs.

"Please let someone with a gun at least catch up to you!" Grace called while she and David sprinted after.

"I brought two of the dogs up to watch the galleries when I came up before," she called back in reassurance. "I'll be— Oh!"

Mrs. Woodward was lying on the floor of the gallery, two large bronze dogs literally sitting on her, but she was unnaturally still. Grace pulled Verity back and saw that the spider on the woman's chest had been chomped in two by one of the dogs.

"Well, that's forty," David breathed.

"Good Dogs," Verity said cheerfully.

****

"Tomorrow. Tea. My house," Verity instructed Grace sternly when she and David left. Grace nodded, forcing a smile, and feeling that she was going to break if she didn't get somewhere alone soon. The constables had been and gone, but with Mrs. Woodward already dead, there was no one to arrest. The guests had left as soon as they decently could, and the servants had been freed from the kitchen where Mrs. Woodward had locked them.

Charlotte was a pillar of strength until Grace insisted that Mrs. Potter take her up to her room, and then Grace ushered the few remaining guests out. Turning around, she realized that she had never seen Pierre leave. There was an empty feeling in realizing that he hadn't said goodbye.

She retreated to the library, where a large chair turned to the corner made an excellent place to curl up and cry. She wasn't sure how much later it was that Pierre found her there.

"I brought you a cup of tea," he said softly. "It seems to be the English response to trauma."

She gurgled a laugh through her tears and took the cup.

"I thought you had left."

He smiled at her a little sadly. "Did you really? I was searching the house and outbuildings for further spiders, bombs, and assassins. It seemed best to be sure."

"It was." She sipped the tea, trying to regain control.

"What is it, love? I know you've been through a great deal today, but I've never seen you so distressed."

Grace thought of what they'd been through together, bitter cold, driving snow, a real risk of freezing to death, and realized that he was right. She took a deep breath. "I'm not pregnant."

His smile lit up his whole face. "Excellent. Then our first can be planned."

"But— You don't want to marry me."

He shook his head. "My foolish love. I've wanted to marry you from the moment when you politely enquired whether I wanted to die when I was considering kissing you." He kissed her forehead and went down on one knee. "Here, let me go about this properly. Grace Elizabeth FitzGeorge, light of my life, sun of my morning and moon of my night, will you do me the inestimable honor of joining your life with mine and marrying me?"

She started laughing and could not stop. He shook a finger at her sternly, although he was still smiling. "I'm still waiting for an answer here."

Her laugher dried up as suddenly as it had started. "But where will we live, and what will we do?"

"We can live anywhere, except France. For then we'd have to kill Napoleon, and I suspect they'd frown on that. But anywhere else. I'd favor America, though, because here we can be whoever we choose to be, even if we were both knighted by the queen."

Grace frowned. "And what about Charlotte? How do I tell her that I'm leaving her? I'm her Lady in Waiting, and I owe her so very much."

Pierre coughed. "Actually, she and I discussed this earlier. Your father wasn't here, and the pageant with the Viscount reminded me that you do have people with a right to worry about your future happiness. I explained my intentions, and she gave her blessings."

Grace crossed her arms. "I don't need anyone's permission, you know. I'm a grown woman."

"I've noticed," he teased.

"And Maine is too cold for me in the winter, really. Why don't we visit your mother in the summer, and live in Boston the rest of the year?"

"Is that a yes?" he asked patiently.

"I'm going to be stuck being a symbol for the rest of my life, and the transition is going to be traumatic as slavery ends, even if it is set to be over seven years. It's an opportunity, and a responsibility, and it would be wrong not to use it."

"My love, I am still on one knee, which is dreadfully uncomfortable, and it has been an extremely long day. Certainly, we can live in Boston. And, certainly, I will help and support you in your work. Yes, we will do our best to make this world a better place. But, please, please put me out of my misery. Grace, will you marry me?"

Grace leaned forward until her lips were a breath from his. "I will," she promised, and kissed him.

The End

Afterword

What change is big enough to cause timelines to diverge? Even a very small event can cause huge changes over time.

In 1563, five years after securing her throne, Elizabeth Tudor of England called a meeting of all the alchemists in England. Only a double handful came. Her methods of dealing with the Catholic supporters of her dead sister, Mary, were a fresh memory. To these few, she laid out a royal command: Stop trying to turn lead into gold.

Impressing upon those present that the secret of turning lead into gold, once found, could never remain hidden, the queen argued that not only would this destabilize the currencies, but also that it would eventually make gold worthless. They would spend their lives on a quest that would only leave them paupers. Instead, she urged, they should look for something more impressive—the spark of life.

Rumors told of lightning captured in a bottle before the birth of Christ. Clocks and similar geared devices existed, movement without direct contact from man. Elizabeth offered the prize of one hundred pounds sterling for the best discovery of each year, and of a thousand pounds additional for the best of each decade.

Lightning was not captured in a bottle during her lifetime, but the sixteenth century saw advances begin. These built on each other, bit by bit, until, by the time of George the Third of England, technology allowed swift enough communication and travel to successfully quell talk of rebellion in the American Colonies.

Medical care improved a bit as well—enough to preserve the king's sister, Elizabeth, from an early death, despite the serious deformities she suffered. Technology grew enough to develop mechanical horses that could run quickly enough to lead to the death of the king's wastrel son, George Prince of Wales, who never became king. Charlotte, queen following the death of George the Third, wed earlier and did not have a breach baby for her first child, so neither she nor the infant died in childbirth. Led by an active queen, instead of a disinterested Regent, England chose to contain Napoleon across the channel rather than to fight him directly.

Many of the minor characters in this novel were real people in our world. I have been as faithful to their memory as the changes in this world permitted. For more on the role of free blacks in society and the abolition movement in America, I recommend the contemporaneous "Appeal to the Coulored Citizens of the World" by David Walker, originally published 1829; "To Plead Our Own Cause: African Americans in Massachusetts and the Making of the Antislavery Movement" by Christopher Cameron, published 2014; and "Generations of Captivity" by Ira Berlin, 2003. Obviously, none of these fine authors is responsible for any errors of interpretation or for any artistic license on my part.

Made in the USA
Middletown, DE
08 January 2016